Murder
&
Malfeasance

(To Kill and Steal)

Errol J Simmons
Dorothy J Morris

Library of Congress Control Number (LCCN): 1-11080455841
ISBN: 978-0-9836488-2-6

Fiction: Contemporary

Published by Errol J Simmons & Dorothy J Morris

Printed in the USA

First Edition - Paperback and Electronic

About the Authors

 **Errol Simmons** was born and raised in Louisiana until drafted into the Army serving a two-year enlistment in Germany. After separating from the military, Errol worked in the Federal civilian workforce until retirement. As a retiree, he resides in Florida, and enjoys gardening and editing the work of other authors.

With a Liberal Arts Degree from Xavier University, writing a novel was on Errol's bucket list, but rose to the top after a few editing jobs. He jokes that a novel was not that easy. His first effort was too short for a novel, but too long for a short story. Dorothy to the rescue.

 **Dorothy J Morris** was born and raised in Fort Lauderdale, Florida but currently resides in Westminster, Maryland. She earned a bachelor's degree from Florida International University and master's degree from McDaniel College.

Dorothy works for the Social Security Administration. She is also the author of three published novels: Fatal Rebounds, Fatal Vengeance, and Fatal Blow. She enjoys writing but spending time with her beautiful granddaughter and mini poodle are equally gratifying. Though, she looks forward to continuing her writing journey. Co-writing a novel with her friend, Errol, was exhilarating.

We hope you enjoy this mystery novel and look forward to your feedback.

This book is dedicated to Andrew Morris, a wonderful husband, father, brother, and friend.

10/11/61 – 04/08/22

RIP

Cyrus Hampton, Director of the Select Committee for General Services, arrived home from work and parked his car in the garage. He entered his home through the garage door and noticed the house was quiet as usual. Shaking away the eeriness, he went into the kitchen to get a bite to eat.

He opened the refrigerator and noticed a freshly made shake in a ninja smoothie cup, encapsulated with a matching lid. A yellow sticky note was attached to the front, which read: *Sorry I couldn't make dinner. Enjoy the smoothie. Will call when I get to Florida.*

Cyrus smiled and made a mental note to thank his wife. He removed the shake from the refrigerator and gulped a large portion. Stomach growling, he sat the fruity drink on the countertop before he retrieved a frozen food meal out of the freezer. Then he retrieved a steak knife out of the kitchen drawer and made a small slit over the plastic portion that contained the vegetables.

After putting the meal in the microwave, he turned on the timer and sat on the stool at the kitchen counter to resume drinking the smoothie. Cyrus pursed his lips with each gulp. He thought the shake was too sweet and grainy but he could not resist the taste of fresh berries. He had consumed half of the smoothie by the time the microwave alerted him that his meal was complete.

His legs felt wobbly when he stood up with the smoothie cup in his hand. Suddenly, a sharp pain pierced through his chest. The pain was so severe, he tumbled over and his body collided with the floor. Coincidentally, the smoothie cup and what was left of the drink splattered all over the kitchen.

Cyrus found it difficult to breathe. He could not think straight. He tried to holler for help but the lack of oxygen in his lungs seemed to strangle him. Crawling like a turtle was the only way he could function.

By the time he made it to the front door and reached up to open it, sweat was protruding down his face and his heart was beating rapidly. He shimmied out the door and onto the porch. "Help!" he screamed but could not hear his voice.

Cyrus managed to crawl down the steps and onto the pathway in front of his home. All of a sudden, his heartbeat slowed and became irregular. He could not move. His eyes flew open before he exhaled and took his last breath.

Chapter 1

Call to Duty

Paul Alexander had just finished a big breakfast of three sausage patties, two boiled eggs, whole wheat toast and his first cup of coffee. The good angel was losing the argument over why he should not help himself to another cup of coffee. *A nice shot of Kalua could be really tasty in that second cup, argued the bad angel.*

His cell phone rang as he started to open the bottle of Kalua. The Caller ID showed it was his friend, Liz, aka Elizabeth Sanchez Varona. She was the second female President of the United States of America, serving the second year of her first term.

"Yes, Madame President." Paul answered her call in a sarcastic but playful tone. "What can I do for you today?"

Liz chuckled. "Paul, that was cold. Do you think I only call when I want something?"

"Of course!" he said in an exaggerated tone.

"Okay, I'm guilty. I need your help, and don't turn me down."

Hearing urgency in her voice, Paul put his coffee cup on the countertop in the kitchen and sat on the edge of the stool.

"I'm sorry, Liz. Let's start over. Good morning, Madame President. How are you this fine morning?"

"Very well, Mr. Paul Alexander, Esquire. How are you?"

"A little hung over, but I'm alert."

"Good. No drinking if you take the job, and I really need you to take the job."

Paul mused while cupping his chin with his thumb and index finger. "Well," he finally replied, "that depends on what the job entails."

"I just learned that Cyrus Hampton, the Director of Select Committee for General Services, died Friday night. The local PDs think the circumstances surrounding his death are suspicious, but they haven't made a determination."

"I am sorry to hear that. How can I help?"

The President paused, before explaining, "The Agency can't run itself. I need someone I know personally, who can pick up where Cyrus left off. No pun intended."

"Liz, why don't you put the Deputy Director in charge until you find a replacement?"

"Eddie Rosenthal is not a good choice at this time."

"Why not?"

"Cyrus told my Senior Advisor that he believed that one or more members of his staff were possibly embezzling government funds, but he did not give any specifics."

2

"Do you believe the Director suspected the deputy was involved?"

"I don't know, which is why I want you to take over as Acting Director."

"I understand your dilemma."

"So…will you take the job? I know you are retired so it'll be temporary, of course."

"For how long?"

"For as long as it takes to find out what the *hell* is going on at SCG."

While pondering Liz' request, Paul stood up and poured himself another cup of coffee with a shot of Kalua. He was single, unemployed, and living off his inheritance. His prior job experience included high-level jobs with the federal government.

Working for the *Select Committee for General Services* sounded appealing. Paul believed it was the perfect opportunity to get back into the workforce even though the job was temporary. Besides, he thought to himself, SCG Headquarters was in Alexandria, Virginia, only thirty-four miles from his home in Brookville, Maryland.

A smile spread across his face as he made up his mind. "Okay, Liz. I'll do it."

"Great," she said with relief. "You can count on Cyrus Hampton's deputy, Eddie Rosenthal, to back you until you become acclimated with the job."

"No, not a good idea."

"And why not, pray tell?"

"You told me the Director suspected at least one of his staff members of embezzling money. As far as I'm concerned, everyone at SCG is a suspect until I can prove otherwise."

"What if I appoint my Senior Advisor, Jimmy Johnson, as your deputy? On a temporary basis, of course. Jimmy already knows the ins and outs of the SCG."

"No!" Paul said a little forcefully than he had intended. "I don't think we would mesh well."

Perplexed, Liz squinted her eyes and stared into space. She had met both Paul and Jimmy in law school, and there never seemed to be any friction between them. She could not help but wonder what made their friendship fizzle. In deep thought, she tried to conjure another person that would be suitable for the job.

"Liz, are you there?" Paul asked after momentary silence.

"Yes, I'm still here. I am trying to think of someone else who knows the Select Committee for General Services better than Jimmy. Do you have anyone in mind?"

"Brian Jeffs. He works in management for the Department of Defense."

"I trust your judgement, Paul. I'll work on getting him transferred to SCG in a couple of weeks. Though, I don't believe the current deputy is going to be happy about it."

"That's his problem."

Liz grinned at Paul's cavalier reply. "I'll call Eddie to relay the news."

"And I'll contact Brian Jeffs in the morning, to offer him the job."

"Paul, you know the Agency's policy. The Director's position requires super high-level security clearance. I will get the ball rolling, so you can report to SCG right away. Stay in touch."

"Sure thing."

After disconnecting the call, Paul took a deep breath and exhaled. He welcomed the opportunity to work again, even if it was for a short period. He was in awe over the prospect of working directly for the President, his best friend since law school almost twenty-five years earlier.

A sheepish grin spread across his face as he realized he was one of few men who could claim that he slept with the President of the United States; albeit they were in their twenties during those occasions. Both had decided early on that their relationship would never blossom into marital bliss. Still, their close bond never withered.

Chapter 2

Awakened

Brian Jeffs heard his house phone ringing near his bed, but he did not want to answer it. It had taken a long time before he was able to drift into a restful night of sleep. Now someone was calling him at three o'clock in the middle of the morning.

On the third ring, he fumbled for the phone on the nightstand. Then he placed the receiver haphazardly against the side of his face, and groggily asked, "Who is this?"

"I need your help," the caller answered, while panting like a thirsty dog.

"What else is new?" Brian grumbled, as he thought the only person that he could ever turn to for help was his best friend and hiking partner, Paul Alexander.

The whining caller stressed, "I wouldn't call you if I didn't need your help."

Rolling his eyes, Brian sat up in bed and turned on the lamp on his nightstand. "What do you want now?"

"I need money."

"What else is new?"

"You're the only family I have."

Sighing, Brian pondered his younger brother and only sibling's last statement. His brother was right. They were the only surviving family members. Their parents died when they were in high school. Soon after, they had transitioned from living in a middle-class household in Boston, Massachusetts, to living with their grandparents in a retirement community in Palm Beach, Florida.

After their grandparents died, Brian went away to college on a full scholarship, and graduated with a degree in Criminal Justice. He began his career as a federal government employee with the Department of Defense and was promoted several times throughout his career.

Brian's brother, on the other hand, stayed in Florida and attended Information Technology school for almost a year before he dropped out and became a functioning alcoholic. He was known for having flashes of brilliance, but he was not inspired to use his intelligence to acquire wealth or prestige. Instead, he was satisfied doing the bare minimum to survive, even if it meant borrowing money he had no intention of repaying.

Shaking his head in disgust, Brian knew his brother would be relentless until he gave him what he wanted. The love of money was his survival tactic, but his brother's dependency on *his money* made him feel like a cash cow.

"C'mon," his brother whimpered. "You know I'll pay you back."

"Like all the other times," Brian sarcastically replied, followed by an audible moan.

"I wouldn't ask for the money if I didn't need it."

"If you had a job, won the lottery, or found a pot of gold, you would still beg for money."

"Don't be like that. I rarely call you."

Massaging his forehead, Brian felt a headache coming on. For as long as he could remember, his brother had been a complete and utter failure. He failed at finding a steady job, failed at finding a permanent place to live, and failed at staying sober.

"Brian, I'm desperate."

"What do you need money for?"

"To get something to eat."

Liar! Brian wanted to scream. He knew his brother needed money to buy alcohol but thought it was fruitless to banter back and forth. Calming his temper, he took a deep breath and exhaled before glancing at the clock on his nightstand.

"Where are you staying?"

"With my girlfriend in Miami."

Brian rolled his eyes. He had never met his brother's girlfriend but could only imagine the hell his brother was putting her through. Covering his mouth while yawning, he knew he needed to end this conversation to get a good night's sleep. "Be at the Western Union in the morning."

"Thanks bro, I appreciate it."

"Sure you do." Brian's tone was laced with cynicism.

After disconnecting the call, Brian laid in bed to try to get some sleep. But he was restless and unnerved by his brother's phone call. Slowly, he climbed out of bed and walked to his office, which was in an adjoining bedroom. He sat at his desk to review the talking points he had prepared for a meeting with the executives and management staff.

Brian viewed this meeting as the catalyst for advancing his career. After starting off as an Analyst at the Department of Defense, he had filled every successive position and worked hard as a Team Leader. He was next in line to become a Branch Chief and wanted to make sure nothing stood in his way.

Now that he was on the right career path, the only thing missing in his life was a decent woman. His co-worker, Maria Hernandez, did not seem to pay him any mind. He did not know much about her, but he was turned on by her exotic looks. Smiling inwardly, Brian visualized her golden-brown complexion and full, plump lips. He was especially enamored with Maria's accent. She spoke English well but with a Spanish undertone.

Nodding with assurance, he thought aloud, "Getting the Branch Chief position will force her to recognize me for the man I am." He spent the next few minutes imagining the status and prestige he would receive from getting the promotion.

Then he snapped out of his spell and turned to his talking points, to refine the details. He went over in his head responses to questions he expected after his presentation. He was so spent, he rested his head on his desk and closed his eyes. Getting promoted and wooing Maria were heavily on his mind when he drifted off to sleep.

Chapter 3

Blindsided

Receiving a call from the President of the United States was always an honor. At least that was what Eddie Rosenthal believed. In light of the Director's untimely death, he had been expecting a call from either Liz or Jimmy Johnson, her Senior Advisor, to tell him he was promoted to the Director's position. He was not surprised when the Administrative Assistant informed him that the President's office was on hold to speak with him.

Eddie had asked himself a series of questions prior to receiving the call. *How should I respond to the President? I think I should accept the Director's position without hesitation, and I should be grateful without fawning. Even though I don't care much for the President, I especially loathe her Senior Advisor. I need to play this right if the latter is calling.*

Jimmy Johnson and I were officers in the Navy – we're the type that would throw anyone under the bus to advance our own careers. I just have to be calm and cool as a sniper. Emotions and body under control at all times. The Director is dead, and I am the best choice to replace him.

Eddie took a deep breath before picking up the phone on his desk and pressing the red indicator button. "Good morning, Madam President," he answered the call in an upbeat voice. "It's an honor to receive your call."

"Good morning Eddie. How are you?"

"I'm fine, considering the circumstances," Eddie replied in a low tone. "It's a shame Cyrus Hampton's life was shortened at such a young age."

Liz nodded. "I agree. My condolences to you, the SCG staff, and the Hampton family."

"Thank you. You can rest assure that I'll do my best to make sure the Agency continues to fulfill its obligations."

"I'm glad you feel that way. However, you don't have to do it alone. I am putting one of my guys in charge temporarily."

"I see." Eddie's voice cracked and his emotions were riddled with disappointment.

"Paul Alexander will be reporting as the Acting Director. He worked as an undercover agent for the FBI in the past, and as a high-level executive for a predecessor government agency before it became the Select Committee for General Services. Mr. Alexander will bring a wealth of experience and knowledge to SCG. He is going to need your help with the transition," Liz added.

"Uh...I'll make sure he gets everything he needs." Eddie's response was insincere yet somber.

"I need you to continue doing a fine job," Liz continued. "You are a great asset to SCG. By the way," she said as an afterthought, "the new Acting Director requested a new deputy, which will be reporting to SCG within the next two weeks."

Eddie paused. His heart began beating rapidly, and sweat bullets suddenly appeared on his forehead. He asked Liz in a shaky voice, "Why are...we getting another deputy? Are you replacing me?"

"No, that is not the case. The new deputy will be an addition to SCG."

"Who is *he*?"

"Brian Jeffs. He works for the Department of Defense."

"I see...um...is there anything else I need to know?"

"You will be reporting to Paul Alexander, until I determine a permanent replacement."

"I understand."

"Thanks again, for your hard work. I'll be in touch."

Eddie held the receiver to his ear long after Liz disconnected the call. He was not a happy camper. For the past five years, he had been the Deputy Director of SCG, and it seemed logical that he would be next in line to be the Director. To add insult to injury, he was asked to work as Co-Deputy Director.

"Well, that was a real kick in the *ass!*" Eddie bellowed, as he slammed the phone on the receiver and slouched in his chair.

All kinds of thoughts were running through his head as he reflected on his conversation with the President. Eddie wondered why the President chose Paul, and not someone who had intimate knowledge of SCG.

Mentally, he said to himself: *I'm sure the President and her Senior Advisor, Jimmy, expect me to be resentful and obstructive. Even though I'm disappointed, I will start off being helpful. I will act like a man determined to earn their trust, respect, and of course, the top job in the very near future – by any means necessary.*

Chapter 4

Doomed

Brian Jeff's eyes flew open when the alarm clock in his bedroom chimed at seven o'clock. "Oh shit! I can't be late this morning!" He dashed out of his home office and into his bedroom at lightning speed.

Understandably, he was chastising himself for not returning to his bedroom, to set the alarm an hour earlier. He showered and dressed. Then he grabbed his suitcoat and briefcase before rushing out of his home. Peering at the digital clock display in his Porsche, Brian believed he had time to make it to the Western Union before heading to work.

He discovered that wiring the money to his brother had taken a lot longer than he had anticipated. He was at the customer service desk in the grocery store, standing behind an older woman who was playing the lottery. She had the cashier manually type her favorite numbers for a dozen tickets. Then she took her precious time rechecking the numbers.

Brian quickly finished the transaction to wire the money to his brother. Then he drove to his office above the speed limit. As he walked down the aisle toward the conference room, he noticed his co-workers on his floor were nowhere in sight. *Of all mornings, everyone appears to be prompt for my meeting. Ain't this a bitch!*

"I'm sorry I'm late," he mumbled, as he entered the conference room and noticed every seat was filled except the one at the head of the sixteen-foot conference table. He filled the vacant chair, then bore a plastered smile while retrieving his talking points from his briefcase.

The Chief Officer, who was also Brian's first-line Supervisor, grumbled, "What took you so long?"

"A family emergency." The last thing Brian wanted to reveal was that his brother was an alcoholic and moocher, always begging for *his* money.

The Chief Officer was unhappy with Brian's response. He folded his arms, leaned slightly back in his chair, and bore a scowl on his face.

Brian scanned his talking points before he stood up and began his presentation. Thirty minutes later, he sat down with a self-assured grin. Then he clasped his hands, sat on the edge of his chair, and asked the attendees if they had any questions.

What happened next eroded his confidence. He was stumped by the number of questions from his Chief Officer. Some questions threw him for a loop. The Q&A session had gotten so bad, Brian stopped talking, slumped back in his chair, and cast a downward gaze. He felt he had been set up to fail, and no answers he could have provided would have sufficed.

His Chief Officer stood up and glared at him. "Brian, I have another meeting right now, but I need you to stop by my office this afternoon. We need to talk about your future with this department."

Brian dropped his head in despair. He was concerned he had failed at the opportunity to impress the Chief Officer with his presentation. He noticed all the meeting attendants had left the conference room except Maria Hernandez, the woman of his dreams.

"Cheer up, Brian," Maria said with a thin smile. "Your presentation wasn't that bad."

"Not according to our Supervisor."

Maria smiled. "It's not the end of the world."

"I suppose you're right." He looked into her deep brown eyes and suddenly, the worry over his present situation was pushed to the background. "Um," he began with renewed spirits, "what are you doing for lunch?"

"I don't have any plans. Why?"

"I would like to take you out to lunch."

Maria paused before speaking. "I don't think that's a good idea."

"Why not?'

"I have my reasons." She stood up and walked out of the conference room, leaving Brian feeling worse than he felt earlier. He slid the talking points in his briefcase before walking to his office.

Pondering his future with the Department of Defense, Brian closed his eyes as he sat behind his desk with heavy shoulders. He suspected the Chief Officer would not recommend him for the promotion that he desperately wanted. Also, his chances of wooing Maria seemed grim.

Chapter 5

Needle in a Haystack

Paul did not expect to be greeted with red carpet and balloons on his first day at the Select Committee for General Services. Though, he had anticipated a level of respect bestowed to anyone in a position of authority. What he received instead, was an icy reception from the staff as he walked through the building and toward his office.

On the top floor of the building, Paul entered his office and approached his Administrative Assistant, which was sitting at a desk several feet from his office. He noted that the woman was middle-aged and appeared professional. Her hair was pulled into a bun, and not a single hair strand was out of place. Everything on her desk was organized and labelled. Even her pens and pencils in the placeholder were pointed in the same direction.

Paul looked at the nameplate on her desk before he greeted her with a smile and an extended hand. "Good morning, Sally Bates, I'm your new Director."

Sally looked up from her computer and stared at him for a few seconds. Then she casted her eyes downward before limply shaking his hand. "Welcome." Her greeting was void of emotion. She returned to her computer, typing on her keyboard as if Paul was not there.

"Okay," he replied with exasperation. "I'll let you know if I need anything."

Paul thought winning Sally over was the least of his worries. She appeared to be good at her job, and that was all that mattered to him.

Upon entering his office, Paul noticed the walls were beige and a large mahogany desk dominated the huge space. He was taken aback for a second, when he eyed the deceased Director's belongings. He made a mental note to tell his Administrative Assistant to box the items and mail them to Cyrus Hampton's family.

Paul took a deep breath before he sat behind the desk to take it all in. Feeling empowered, he reclined in the oversized, executive office chair. Then he clasped his hands on the back of his head and closed his eyes. His purpose for being at the Select Committee for General Services never escaped him. Paul was determined to find out whether any shenanigans were being carried out by SCG staff members.

"Uh, excuse me," the SCG Deputy Director said, after he cleared his throat and stepped into Paul's office.

Paul's eyes slowly opened as he sat up in his chair. He tilted his head to one side before asking the uninvited visitor, "What can I do for you?"

"I'm sorry for barging in. Your door was open, so I decided to come in to introduce myself. My name is Eddie Rosenthal, your Deputy Director."

Grinning, Paul stood up and shook Eddie's extended hand. "Nice to meet you. You are the one person I wanted to meet. Please close the door and have a seat," he said as he pointed to one of the two chairs on the opposite side of the desk.

Eddie selected the chair closest to the door. Then he sat on the edge of the chair and bore a plastered smile. "It's nice to finally meet you. Welcome to SCG."

"Thank you." Paul nodded after noting Eddie's smile did not match his words. Pensively, he analyzed his Deputy's demeanor. He gathered Eddie had a chip on his shoulder but did not know why.

"It's so nice to meet you," Eddie said with a forced smile. Is there anything you would like to know about SCG?"

"I'm already familiar with the SCG. I'm just here temporarily, at least until the President appoints a permanent Director."

"Well, I'm here to help you in any capacity."

"I'm glad to know this. I guess you can start by getting me the personnel files for every SCG staff member."

Eddie frowned. "Why is that necessary? I know the SCG staff well. I can tell you anything you need to know."

"The personnel files in addition to any information you can provide will give me insight about each employee."

"I still don't see why the files are necessary."

"Well," Paul began in a deliberate tone, "your former Director approached you about possible fraudulent activity here at SCG."

"I thought that matter was laid to rest. The audit trail Cyrus Hampton had ordered did not confirm his suspicions."

"That may be the case, but I want to make sure we are doing everything possible to combat fraud or the appearance of fraud. How soon can you get me those personnel files?"

"Personnel files are electronic." Eddie eyed the computer monitor on Paul's desk, before adding, "It shouldn't be a problem for you to get direct access."

"I need hard copies of the files. Is that a problem?"

I'm not your damn Administrative Assistant! Eddie wanted to scream. Instead, he chose a conciliatory response. "We have a lot of employees, and it will take some time."

"Maybe you can stagger my request by giving me twenty files at a time. Is that doable?"

Eddie nodded, struggling to control his internal anger.

"Terrific!" Paul replied with overzealous enthusiasm. "Start pulling the files for the Administrative staff first."

"Is that it?"

"I want to meet with the entire SCG staff in fifteen minutes. Please notify everyone."

That's not my job!! Eddie wanted to shout. Instead, he bore a thin smile and nodded. "Sure thing. I'll ask the Administrative Assistant to tell everyone to meet in the multipurpose room on the first floor."

"Great. I'll see you there."

Eddie stood up and turned toward the door. Suddenly, he turned around and bit his bottom lip.

Paul noticed Eddie staring at him and shuffling his feet. "Is there anything you need to tell me?"

"Uh...I was told you requested another Deputy Director."

"Yes, I did. His name is Brian Jeffs. We are arranging his transfer from the Department of Defense."

"Um...what role will he play?"

"We can sit down and figure out the logistics once Mr. Jeffs reports to SCG. Don't worry, you can be assured that your role and responsibilities will not be impacted."

"Thank you. I appreciate that." Eddie's tension dissipated. Though, the appointment of Paul Alexander as the Acting Director had gotten under his skin. He knew he had to make a better effort of concealing his true feelings.

***

When Eddie left his office, Paul mulled over his opinions about his deputy. He noticed his subordinate's disposition varied during their brief conversation. Paul had detected bitterness when he shook Eddie's hand, he detected fearfulness when he told Eddie about exploring Cyrus Hampton's allegation of fraud, and he detected resoluteness after he assured Eddie that his current job was not in jeopardy.

Paul retrieved a pad and pen from his desk and jotted a note to review Eddie's personnel file as soon as possible. Then he put on his suit jacket and headed to the multipurpose room.

Chapter 6

Lucky Break

Feeling deflated and embarrassed by his performance at the meeting, Brian remained in his office the rest of the morning. He did not want to be the target of jeers from his colleagues. But he cheered up when his cell phone rang, and the Caller ID showed it was his friend.

"Hey Paul, what's up?"

"I'm going to cut to the chase. I want you to work for me."

Brian's mouth flew open and his eyes widened as he sat up in his chair. "Are you serious? Where…when…what will I be doing?" He was excited but cautious.

"I've been appointed as the Acting Director of the Select Committee for General Services. You will be one of my deputies."

"Select Committee for General Services?" I've never heard of them. Which cabinet department owns them?

"Actually, they are not under a cabinet head."

"So they are an independent Agency?"

"Yes, the SCG was formed under a former President, and successive Presidents retained the Agency for their purposes. You can say it's the President's baby."

"Okay, and what does the President's baby do?"

"The SCG provides support to former spy agents and government officials. Basically, we create new identities and official government documents that correspond with the new identities. We also provide cover when creating employment histories so former spy agents can get pensions once they are eligible."

"Awesome. Sounds interesting. Count me in."

"Glad to hear this."

Out of curiosity, Brian asked, "What happened to the former SCG Director?"

"He's dead. Do you want the job?"

Brian frowned after hearing about the status of the former Director. Though, his face brightened and his eyes sparkled over the prospect of getting a higher position with another agency. Considering his failed performance at his presentation earlier, his answer was a no-brainer. "Paul, I would love to work for you. When do I start?"

"In the next week or two."

"That soon?"

"Is that a problem?"

"No, but what about my current job?"

"Don't worry about that. I figured you would accept the job offer so someone is arranging your transfer."

"How did you pull that off?"

"I'll fill you in on a need-to-know basis. I'll be the Director of SCG on a temporary basis, but I'll make sure your job becomes permanent before I leave. Are you in agreement with these terms?"

"That's fine with me. I can't thank you enough."

"Don't thank me yet. The current SCG Deputy may not like the idea of someone else sharing the same title. But don't worry, you will be working directly with me to solve a matter I've been asked to investigate."

"I understand. Is there anything else I should know?"

Paul chuckled. "Yeah, don't make me regret my decision."

"You know me better than that."

Paul smiled. "That's why I chose you. I'll be in touch."

"Thank you."

"No problem."

After disconnecting the call, Brian sat back in his office chair with a huge grin on his face. He realized the opportunity to work for SCG would be even better than the promotion he wanted at the Department of Defense. He would get a fresh start in a new workplace, and he would be working for his best friend and hiking partner.

Brian was gloating over the prospect of working for SCG when the Executive Secretary entered his office. He was puzzled when she stood there in silence. "Can I help you?"

"The Chief Officer wants to see you in his office, right away."

Brian figured his Supervisor wanted to speak with him about his presentation. In a cynical tone, he asked, "Did he say what he wanted?"

"I'm afraid not," the Executive Secretary said in a hushed whisper. Though, she assumed it was about rumblings of Brian's failed presentation.

"Okay, I'll be there soon."

Brian was about to freak out, but it dawned on him that his best friend had arranged his transfer and automatic promotion to Deputy Director at the Select Committee of General Services. Anything his Supervisor had to say to him would be pointless.

Chin up and chest out, Brian stood up, put on his suit jacket. Then he walked to his Supervisor's office feeling transformed.

"You asked to speak with me," Brian said as soon as he arrived at his destination.

The Chief Officer looked up from a document he was reviewing on his desk. "Have a seat. Brian. This isn't going to take long."

"I'd rather stand, if you don't mind."

"Suit yourself," the Chief Officer said before he folded his hands and leaned toward Brian with twisted lips. "I was not impressed with your presentation this morning. So I decided to recommend Maria Hernandez for the Branch Chief position."

Brian was at a loss for words. Maria had only been a Team Leader for a year, and he was the one who trained her. His thoughts drifted back to his earlier encounter with her. *She knew it! She knew she was going to get the promotion. That's probably why she turned down my lunch invitation.*

"I'm happy for her," Brian managed to say, after recovering from this new revelation.

"I need all hands-on-deck to help Maria transition to her new position. You will be responsible for all of her work until I can find another Team Leader to replace her."

Brian was about to object when the phone on his Supervisor's desk began ringing.

The Chief Officer looked at the Caller ID and seemed to panic. "I have to take this call," he told Brian, before answering the phone with a sense of urgency.

Brian noticed that whoever was on the other end of the call did not give his Supervisor the opportunity to offer a proper greeting. In fact, the Chief Officer appeared at a loss for words during the thirty second conversation.

The call ended as abruptly as it began. The Director hung up the phone and looked at his subordinate through slanted eyes.

"What's going on?" Brian asked but already had an inkling.

"I think you already know."

"I'm not sure. Why don't you tell me?" Brian folded his arms and smirked.

"You are being transferred to another federal government agency."

"Really?" Brian mused. He was reveling in the moment. "Did they say which government entity?"

"I'm not privy to that information, but apparently someone has already contacted you and offered you the position."

"And I accepted." Brian's response was unyielding and flippant.

The Chief Officer cleared his throat after feeling uneasy with his inability to control Brian's destiny. "Um...someone from Personnel will be contacting you soon with specifics on your transfer."

"That's good to know. Do you need me for anything else?"

"No, you may be excused."

Brian smiled from ear-to-ear as he left his Supervisor's office. He was thrilled when he noticed Maria walking in his purview. Biting his bottom lip, he mentally undressed her through lust-filled eyes. He loved the way her black flair skirt showed off her muscular but feminine legs, the way her bright red lipstick adorned her plump lips, and the way her tight-fitting blouse outlined her small, perky breasts, which bounced with every step she took in his direction.

"Hello Maria," he said, while gazing into her beautiful, dark brown eyes. "I just heard about your promotion. Congratulations!"

"Um...thank you. I wanted to tell you earlier, but I didn't want things to be awkward between us."

"Now that I know, can I take you out to lunch?"

"Are you sure there are no hard feelings? I mean…I knew how badly you wanted the promotion. Everyone knew."

"Come on, Maria. We're not in grade school. Besides, I have great news to share with you."

Maria smiled. "Sure, we can go to lunch together but not today. I have to meet with our Supervisor to discuss my new duties."

"How about dinner?"

"Are you asking me out on a date?"

"Yeah."

Maria hesitated before a smile spread across her face. "Okay, Brian. Give me your cell phone."

Brian did not hesitate as he retrieved his phone from his suit pocket and handed it to her.

Maria inserted her name and phone number as a contact in Brian's cell phone, then she handed it back to him. "We can make plans for a dinner date when you call me. Send me a text message, so I can add you as a contact. I don't want to accidentally ignore your call."

"Most definitely." Brian watched as Maria turned around, sashay down the aisle, and out of his sight.

Bursting with excitement, he sauntered to his office and closed the door behind him. He had accomplished two things in less than one hour. Brian had been promoted to Deputy Director for SCG, which was equivalent to being a Branch Chief at the Department of Defense, and he had asked Maria

Hernandez out on a date. *Life could not get any better*, he thought to himself.

Chapter 7

On Edge

Over one hundred SCG staff members were already seated in the conference room when Paul walked in looking like a man on a mission. He approached the podium and retrieved the microphone from the stand. Then he scanned the audience and took note of their icy cold stares. It was obvious to him that he was not liked, and possibly hated.

Paul reasoned that his stay at the Select Committee for General Services was temporary, so he was not there to make friends. He focused on one goal and that was to either affirm or negate the suspicion of fraud at SCG.

Clearing his throat, he began the meeting in a strong, authoritative tone: "Good morning, everyone. My name is Paul Alexander, your Acting Director. I'm here because Cyrus Hampton, died unexpectedly and the President of the United States asked me to come to the Agency temporarily until she appoints a permanent Director. She approached me because quick action was needed, and she knows I have the background and experience necessary to run this complex and sensitive operation."

Complete silence from the attendees made the room feel stark and cold. There was not even a pin drop. Paul thought to himself, *Luckily, my military background prepared me for awkward moments.*

"Now, on a personal level," Paul continued his speech, trying to sound chipper. "I have a law degree, worked for several elected officials, and served as both Deputy Director and Director for several government agencies. I am very familiar with SCG, as I have worked for its predecessor Agency in the past.

My presence at SCG is to make sure we carry out the Agency's mission. I want to assure you that your roles and responsibilities will not change. The work you do here is important, and I want to make sure we continue producing quality products and results. I also want to ensure that we do everything in our power to combat *fraud,* inside and outside SCG."

Paul allowed the last statement to stand by itself for a few seconds, before continuing, "I have an open-door policy, but I encourage you to follow the proper protocol by speaking with your first-line Supervisor beforehand.

Periodically, I may invite some of you to my office to brief me on various matters. In addition to the current Deputy, Eddie Rosenthal, you will also be working with a new Deputy Director, Brian Jeffs. He will be joining us in a couple of weeks."

Audible gasps were followed by deafening silence. Paul scanned the room for a few seconds, before asking, "Does anyone have any questions?"

Paul looked at Eddie on the front row, who avoided eye-contact. Then he surveyed the room and was surprised no one raised their hands. "This concludes our meeting. Feel free to let me know if you have any questions." He returned the mic to its stand and left the room.

Several SCG staff members gathered around their Deputy Director, who remained seated. "What happened?" one employee asked Eddie. "I thought you were going to get Cyrus Hampton's position."

A bewildered Eddie shrugged his shoulders and threw his hands in the air as if surrendering.

Another employee asked, "Who is this Paul person? Where did he come from?"

Eddie said, "He's only the Acting Director."

"Well, I don't like him," a senior employee chimed in.

"Give him a chance. He seems nice." Eddie tried to sound upbeat but failed miserably. "Let's wait to see what's going to happen." He stood up and walked toward the exit, leaving behind perplexed employees.

***

Paul stopped by the Personnel office to finish completing paperwork for his transition to the Select Committee for General Services. Then he went to lunch with a young lady he had met a week earlier. He discovered they really didn't have anything in common other than physical attraction.

When he returned to his office, his Administrative Assistant was nowhere in sight. He assumed she went home early, so he decided to follow her lead.

He put on his suit jacket and took the elevator to the garage located on the ground floor of the building. Then he headed to his sports BMW. He stopped in mid-stride after discovering he had a flat tire.

Paul's car was practically brand new and fully loaded with all the bells and whistles. The tire indicator light would have flashed on if air in his tire was low. He could not help but believe this was foul play, while looking around to see if any suspects were nearby. Reflexively, he retrieved his cell phone from his front coat pocket and called AAA.

An hour later, the tow truck came to his rescue. The tow driver found that there were no punctures in Paul's tire after he inflated it with an air pump.

Eddie spotted Paul and the tow truck after he exited the building. "What's going on?" he asked Paul.

"Flat tire."

"Do you need a ride?"

Paul hesitated before responding, "No, I'm okay. The tow truck driver is almost done here."

"Okay, I'll see you tomorrow."

Paul nodded in response. His instincts about the Deputy Director were not good. For a split second, he wondered if Eddie was the culprit that flattened his tire. That idea, however, was debunked after he realized the perpetrator could have been any one of the SCG staff members that gave him icy stares all day.

He tipped the tow truck driver, climbed behind the wheel of his car, and headed home. Then he shook his head and chuckled to himself. *Why am I blaming anyone for the flat tire? Maybe it was just a fluke.*

Chapter 8

Pity Party

Eddie did not know how to feel about Paul's flat tire. He had a feeling it was not an accident. In a way, he felt vindicated since he did not get promoted to the Director's position. But he was still bitter after realizing the flat tire was easily fixed. He was in a bad mood when he returned home from work.

After parking his car in the garage of his modest four-bedroom, two-and-a-half-bathroom home, Eddie walked through the garage door and headed to the kitchen. Then he grabbed a six-pack of Coors beer from the refrigerator, placed it on the countertop, and plopped down on the kitchen stool. He drank one can of beer in less than a minute before grabbing a second one.

"What are you doing?" his wife, MaryJo, asked as she entered the kitchen.

Eddie's back was to her as he answered, "I'm drinking my sorrows away." Then he drank the second can of beer in four big gulps. Eddie bore a thin smile before he grabbed a third can of beer and walked into the living room.

MaryJo followed Eddie in the living room and peered into her husband's sad eyes. "Honey, what's wrong?"

Sitting in his recliner, Eddie used the remote to the 55-inch flat screen TV to turn to the ESPN sports channel. He was looking for a distraction, any distraction that would take his mind off work.

"Honey, talk to me," MaryJo pleaded, as she sat across from Eddie on the living room sofa. "What's going on?"

"I'm fine."

"I know you, Eddie. You're not fine." MaryJo stood up, took the remote from her husband's hand and turned down the volume. Then she pensively stared into his eyes after returning to the sofa.

Eddie sighed. "I have a new Director, but he's only temporary. He reported to work today. I like him, don't get me wrong. But he doesn't know the job like I do."

MaryJo nodded in understanding. "Maybe you can talk to him about how you're feeling."

"For what?" Eddie grimaced. "It's not going to change anything."

"I know, but maybe you can get an understanding of how he was selected over you."

"I don't know if that'll do any good."

"Didn't you tell me he was in that position on a temporary basis? You know there's still a possibility that you will get the Director's job."

"I thought about that, but I'm not convinced that I'm being considered for the promotion."

Finishing off the third can of beer, Eddie's voice cracked as he recited in a woeful tone, "It has been a long journey from being the son of a farmer. As a young man, I learned dad was deep in debt because crop prices did not cover the expenses." He paused, before continuing, "You know...a small farm not well-managed is a money pit, especially when you have two kids to feed. It's no wonder mom and dad drank way too much."

Eddie turned to his wife and asked, "Did I tell you my dad died after driving a tractor while intoxicated?"

MaryJo nodded. She heard this story over a hundred times, and only when her husband was heavily drinking. She sat back on the sofa, listening to his every word.

Staring into space while carrying on with his storytelling session, Eddie sorrowfully explained, "Mom couldn't take the pressure because her skills at running the farm were poorer than dad's. When she killed herself, she left me and my brother parentless. Mom planned her death carefully, leaving us with her parents."

Eddie paused, before explaining, "We were not home when mom took the overdose. So it was natural that we stayed with our grandparents. I no longer viewed farming as a fun business. That's why I seriously considered joining the Navy as soon as I graduated from high school. My grandparents talked me out of it and convinced me to go to the Pollard Naval Institute. I really miss them."

Eddie stood up and walked into the kitchen to grab another can of beer. Then he opened the can and took a huge gulp before returning to the recliner in slow motion. His voice slurred when he spoke again. "I served…this country…for almost twenty…years before I started my career with SCG. I…deserve the Director's job."

MaryJo leaned over and patted him on the knee. "Cheer up, honey. There's still hope."

"I hope you're right."

Eddie forced a smile, but his heart was not at ease. More than once, he wondered if his former Director had suspected him of committing fraud at SCG. *Is this why I did not get the promotion?* he thought to himself. At that very moment, Eddie became determined to do whatever necessary to make sure Paul did not come close to discovering he was involved in fraudulent activity.

Chapter 9

Cherry on Top

Brian was feeling good about becoming the new SCG Co-Deputy Director. What started the day as bad news with a disruptive phone call from his brother, concluded with him being granted a promotion at another federal government agency. Things could have turned out differently had it not been for Paul offering him the job with SCG.

To add the cherry on top, Brian had managed to secure a date with Maria. She had readily accepted a date when he called her on her cell phone. She seemed happy to hear from him, and he was equally happy to hear her voice.

"I look forward to our date," she told him in a sultry tone.

"Me too."

Brian bore a fresh buzz cut and he was smelling good after spraying his neck and wrist with Valentino cologne. He was hoping to impress Maria in his dark gray two-piece Armani suit, white-collar dress shirt, and silk black tie.

Taking one final look in the mirror, Brian grabbed his house keys and fob to his new Porsche sports car. Then he drove forty-five minutes to Maria's condominium in Falls Church, Virginia. Her condo was newly constructed and located in a quaint, historic neighborhood.

After parking the Porsche in front of the building that housed Maria's condo unit, Brian climbed out and walked in the lobby area. He pressed the elevator to go to the second floor.

A big smile spread across his face when the elevator door opened and Maria appeared in his view. She always made him feel giddy inside, like a schoolboy every time he was in her presence.

"Hello, Maria. I was headed upstairs to meet you."

"I know," she said as she bolted pass him, "but I thought I would make your life easier by meeting you downstairs."

Brian walked quickly to catch up with her. "It's no rush."

"I know, Papi," Maria replied with a big smile. Her plump lips were magnified with bright red lipstick. "But I'm hungry."

Papi! Brian loved the way she greeted him. He made a mental note to not be upset with his brother the next time he called begging for money. He hurriedly opened the passenger door of his car. Then he stood back to watch Maria climb in the seat and buckle up. Feeling invigorated, he threw a fist pump in the air as he strolled to the driver's side of his car and climbed behind the steering wheel.

"Where are we going for dinner?" Maria asked, after Brian buckled up.

"It's a surprise."

Maria waited for Brian to start the ignition and exit her condo complex, before asking, "Do you have a new job lined up?"

Brian glanced in her direction with a raised brow. "Why do you ask?"

"I heard you were leaving the Department of Defense." Maria did not mention that the Chief Officer told her about Brian's transfer in confidence.

Brian grinned. "Well…you're looking at the next Deputy Director of Select Committee for General Services."

"Are you serious?" Maria asked in awe.

Brian nodded. "I report to SCG in two weeks."

"I'm so happy for you," she sincerely responded.

Maria was not attracted to Brian or interested in him in any way. She had worked hard for the Branch Chief position at the Department of Defense, but she did not like doing whatever it took to keep her position. The promotion was temporary with the likelihood of becoming permanent. Of course, the permanent status was contingent on Maria's willingness to continue sleeping with the Chief Officer.

Glancing at Brian, Maria smiled and started looking at him differently. In light of learning about his new position with SCG, she believed Brian might be her only hope of escaping her Supervisor's sexual advances.

Brian drove to *Estadio*, a Spanish bistro near the Capital in DC. The restaurant served traditional Spanish cuisines. "I hope you like what's on the menu," he told Maria after the waiter escorted them to a table near the window.

"I'm sure I will. I love Spanish food."

After they were seated, Maria reached across the table and placed her hand on top of Brian's. Then she gazed longingly into his eyes. "I can't wait to see what's on your menu." She winked at him to let him know she was not talking about food.

Brian's heart was beating so fast, he started to stutter when the waiter asked for their drink orders. "I…um…."

"We want," Maria intervened, "your finest red wine." Then she looked over at Brian, and asked, "Is that okay with you?"

Brian blushed.

After the waiter served them wine in crystal flutes, he took their food orders and excused himself. There was momentary silence after the waiter left, so Maria leaned toward Brian and spoke in a suggestive tone. "I must say," she began, "I was surprised when you asked me out."

"Well, it wasn't for my lack of trying. It seems you always found a reason to reject my requests in the past. What changed your mind this time?"

"The thought of not seeing you at work." Maria batted her eyes, before adding, "I don't like having relationships with my colleagues."

Brian nodded. "I understand."

Maria justified her half-truth by rationalizing that the relationship with the Chief Officer was a business decision. She believed she could have a similar relationship with Brian. Though, she started to view him in a different light, especially after comparing him to all the other men she dealt with in the past.

After assessing Brian's physical characteristics, Maria was impressed with his tall but muscular build, his beautiful but imperfect smile, and his deep dimples. Everything else about him screamed, "I am a nerd but I have swag." Maria began to nod and grin. *I think he's a keeper*, she thought to herself.

"So Brian," Maria said with a twinkle in her eyes, "please tell me more about SCG. I know it's a mysterious Agency. Is it true that SCG reports directly to the President?"

Brian nodded. "Yes, SCG is a branch of the White House. Unfortunately, I can't tell you more than what you already know."

"That's too bad. I would love to work for you some day."

Brian smirked. "You never know."

On that note, Maria stood up, leaned across the table, and planted a juicy kiss on Brian's lips. "I hope this won't be the last time you ask me out on a date." She sat in her chair and gazed at Brian with a look of yearning.

Brian was caught off guard but he had 'happy' written all over his face. "Well…," he began after clearing his throat, "I…uh…I'm looking for something more permanent."

"Are you asking to go steady with me?"

"I would love to go steady with you. How do you feel about it?"

Maria put her hand under the table, reached over and touched between Brian's legs and massaged his manhood. "Does this answer your question?"

Clearly aroused, Brian began breathing heavily. Maria was turning him on in the middle of the restaurant. His eyes rolled up, as he replied in a high-pitch voice, *"Yes!!"*

Maria giggled. "I'm glad we'll be seeing more of each other."

"Me too." Brian smiled to himself, feeling as though he was closer to making Maria his wife -- in the very near future.

Chapter 10

Something's Amiss

Now that Paul was working as the Acting SCG Director, he had more of an incentive to adapt to a healthy lifestyle. The next morning, he had herbal tea, whole wheat cereal, almond milk, fruit, and two medjool dates with a second cup of tea.

Looking down at his waist, Paul believed he was losing weight but was afraid to get on the scale. "No guilt and no pain," he recited to himself.

His cell phone rang just as he washed out his cup and placed it in the drying rack. It was Liz again - based on his Caller ID. He answered her call with a wide grin. "How are you, beautiful?"

"I'm wonderful. How is my handsome man?" A smile followed her flirty but rhetorical question.

Paul snickered. "Why is it that as of late, I've been getting your calls as soon as I finish breakfast? Do you have cameras in my house?" he teased.

Liz grinned. "No, we are just in sync. Were you expecting a call from another special person?"

"Only yours," Paul replied with a deep, sexy voice.

"You're such a liar." Liz threw her head back and chuckled. "I'm certain you've had several dates since we last spoke."

"Well, if you must know - I had a lunch date yesterday, but it's nothing serious."

"Don't tell me – she has a big butt and small boobs, right?" Liz knew her friend well. Any woman, attractive or not, had a chance with Paul, as long as she met his shallow criteria.

"C'mon Liz. It was just a lunch date. You know you're the only one for me." Beaming, Paul was clearly enthralled in their playful banter.

"I so believe you not. But a little lie in the morning is good for the ego."

"Okay, enough of the niceties. I know you're not calling to get the scoop on my dating life."

"You're right." Liz paused before explaining in a sorrowful tone, "I'm afraid I've gotten you into a mess. I just found out Cyrus Hampton was murdered. The disturbing thing is the method. We may be dealing with a cold-blooded, sociopath who planned the Director's demise with precision."

Perplexed, Paul asked, "What are you talking about?"

"During our first conversation, I told you the Police thought Cyrus' death was suspicious. According to the 911 operator, his neighbors reported he had a heart attack. But the Emergency room doctors discovered signs that he may have been poisoned. The hospital sent samples of his blood to the toxicologist and they found a quantity of red dye and berries in his esophagus."

Paul's brows furrowed, while asking, "Are you trying to tell me he was poisoned with berries?"

"Yeah. It turns out the berries are toxic in the winter when white, but edible in late spring and summer when red. Babe, this is summer!!!"

Paul's eyes widened after thinking about what the President told him. "Are you saying the berries were white?"

"Yes. The FBI is investigating how many people know about this type of berry, and where they came from. I wonder how the killer got Cyrus to eat them, actually - drink them. Evidently, they were mixed in his smoothie." The President paused, before admitting, "This is some scary shit."

Cupping his chin, Paul took a deep breath and exhaled. He mulled over the new revelation of Cyrus' demise and could not help but wonder about his own safety.

"Are you there?" the President asked after she was met with silence.

"Uh...yeah...I'm here."

"The FBI is on the case. Agents may be showing up at SCG to ask the staff some questions." Liz hesitated before pondering her next statement. "Paul, I would understand if you no longer wanted the job."

"Of course, I want the job," Paul replied. Though, his stomach rumbled from nervous jitters. "I have always loved a good mystery."

"Books are harmless. This is real death."

"You're right. It pales in comparison to getting a flat tire on your first day at work."

Alarmed, Liz sat up on the edge of her chair. "What are you talking about?"

"It's not a big deal. I just needed an air pump to inflate my tire."

"Okay…if you say so." Liz was leery of Paul's cavalier reply. "But I do have good news."

"Pray tell."

"Top Secret Security clearance for your new deputy should be finalized by the end of the week. As we speak, the Department of Defense is arranging Brian Jeffs' transfer to SCG."

"That's good to hear. My buddy is going to be a great asset to SCG. He's smart and catches on quickly." Paul smirked, before asking, "Did I tell you Brian's brother has awesome computer skills that can hack into banks?"

"As we are both attorneys, I did not hear that. I am certain the US Government has contractors and attorneys that can obtain bank records with properly executed warrants."

Paul cracked up laughing.

"Good to hear you are still on board. Watch your *ass*." Liz hung up without saying goodbye as usual.

Paul shook his head and sniggered. Then he grabbed his suit jacket and headed for work. He was thinking about his conversation with the President during the drive. He did not tell Liz that the cause of Cyrus' death had caused him to have trepidations about working for SCG. Paul was curious about why the Director was targeted. He also wondered if he would end up in the same predicament.

Chapter 11

The Big Reveal

Upon entering the Select Committee for General Services' headquarters on day two, Paul greeted staff members in his peripheral view with a nod and a thin smile. He did not wait or expect to be greeted in-kind. He headed to his office with caution, especially after learning the former Director was murdered.

Paul noted that his Administrative Assistant was not at her desk. He brows furrowed after he noticed his Deputy Director standing in front of his office with an arm full of files.

"Good morning," Eddie said in a jovial tone. "How are you this *fine* morning?" He was laying it on thick but did not care. Getting a promotion to the Director's position after Paul's temporary stint was his goal. *If kissing ass is the path to success – so be it.*

"I'm fine, Eddie." Paul's tone was short and flat. "What can I do for you?"

"I have the first batch of personnel files you requested." With pearly white teeth on full display, Eddie held out the files in Paul's direction.

"Thanks." Paul grabbed the files and pushed past Eddie to enter his office. He sat behind his desk and opened the first file on top of the batch. Paul knew Eddie was trying to kiss up to him, but he learned from vast experience to never trust a brown-noser.

"Is there anything else you need?" Eddie persisted, his voice sounded strained and unrelenting.

"That'll be all for now." Paul looked up from the file as Eddie turned to exit his office. "There is one thing you should know. The FBI may be stopping by the office, so make sure you tell the staff that their cooperation is necessary."

"May I ask why they're coming?"

"They are investigating Cyrus Hampton's death. They have reason to believe he was murdered."

Eddie's mouth flew open, and his right hand soared to his chest. He appeared shocked by this revelation. "Did...you... say...murdered?"

"Yes."

"Do they have any suspects?"

"Not that I know of."

"Okay. I'll put everyone on alert. Anything else?"

Paul nodded in the affirmative. "Can you tell me who is responsible for operating the SCG database?"

"The Information Technology Center oversees the SCG database. Barrett Pike is the Team Leader in that department."

"That's good to know. Please inform Barrett that I would like to meet him later on today."

"Will do."

"I'd appreciate it." Paul's eyes averted to the batch of files, as he mumbled, "Please close the door behind you." He kept his eyes focused on the file, making it clear that their exchange was over.

When Eddie walked out the office, Paul perused through the files and noticed his deputy's personnel file was not included the batch. He made a mental note to ask his Administrative Assistant to retrieve the file from the HR department. There was something off-kilter about their last conversation that piqued his interest.

***

When Eddie left the Director's office, he realized his attempt at kissing up to his new boss had failed, miserably. He vowed to think of another ploy to win Paul over. In the meantime, he relayed Paul's message to the IT Team Leader. Then he called a quick meeting with the SCG staff to convey information about Cyrus Hampton's death.

He waited for everyone to be seated in the conference room, before explaining, "I recently learned that our former Director was murdered. I need everyone to cooperate when the FBI arrives at SCG." Eddie sighed, before asking, "Does anyone have any questions?"

Tameka Collins-Brown, the HR Team Leader, asked, "Why are they coming here?"

"To investigate the mystery of why Cyrus was murdered."

"How do they know he was murdered?" she asked with wrinkled brows.

"I don't have the exact answer to that question, but I assume an autopsy was performed." Eddie looked around the room, before asking, "Are there any other questions?"

One of the senior writers, Stephanie McPherson, raised her hand before standing up. "Do you think they suspect one of us of murdering him?"

Eddie shrugged. "I'm not privy to that information."

Barrett Pike, the IT Team Leader, stood up and shouted, "For God's sake! You call us to this meeting to tell us the FBI is investigating Cyrus Hampton's murder, and you can't provide any details. What type of nonsense is this! The FBI's mere presence here at SCG will send the wrong message to our clients, and you know it."

"Please calm down," Eddie said with an extended hand. "I understand your concern, but, unfortunately, I'm just the messenger." Eddie knew there was nothing he could do to calm the IT Team Leader once he got fired up. He also knew Barrett was probably nervous about his impending meeting with the Director.

"This is ridiculous!" Barrett stormed out of the conference room in a rage, but the remaining staff lingered around a little longer asking Eddie questions he could not answer.

Ten minutes later, everyone cleared the room except Eddie. He remained seated, mulling over Tameka Collins-Brown's question: *How do they know Cyrus Hampton was murdered?* Eddie thought that was a good question. He was hung up on the fact that the news stations had reported earlier that Cyrus had a heart attack.

Chapter 12

Youngblood

Barrett Pike was the youngest staff member at SCG. He was recruited to work as the IT Team Leader after graduating at the top of his class from an Ivy League school. For the past five years, he worked with a small staff to maintain the SCG database. He and his staff had built automation tools that made it easier to process new identities and evidentiary documents. His team also enacted programmatic measures to ensure pensioners created by SCG staff received their retirement checks on time.

The upcoming meeting with Paul had him on edge. To add to his uneasiness, Barrett was flabbergasted after learning how Cyrus Hampton died. "How do they know for sure he was murdered?" he whispered aloud, as he sat in his office chair cupping his chin and pondering this revelation.

Barrett was not necessarily worried about the FBI questioning him about Cyrus Hampton's death. But his personal life was in shambles. A bad gambling habit was not only expensive, but it also forced him into compromising situations. An interview with the FBI was sure to open a can of worms and worsen problems with his debtors. At least that was what he believed.

After checking his watch, Barrett put on his suit jacket and headed downstairs to the computer room. He wanted to alert his team of his impending meeting with the Director. To his surprise, Paul was in the computer room talking with some of the IT staff.

"Uh…hello," Barrett muttered as he approached Paul with an extended hand.

Paul turned to Barrett and shook his hand. "Nice to meet you. I was headed to your office for our meeting but took a detour to the computer room. If you don't mind, I would like for your IT expert to finish explaining how the SCG system works."

"Uh…that's not necessary. I'll explain it to you," Barrett insisted, as he dismissed the IT expert with a side-nod.

"Okay, lead the way," Paul said, as he directed his attention to the computer galley.

"Is there anything specific that you need to know?"

"I need to know everything about the SCG database."

Over the next hour, Barrett walked Paul through the ins and outs of the SCG system, while demoing multiple processes. He also answered many questions about the process for retaining data on retired pensioners, especially those created by SCG staff.

This spiel was not new to Barrett. He had given his former Director the same presentation. The difference was Paul was asking specifics about the application process for pensioners. "Is there anything else you would like to know?" he asked, in an attempt to end the impromptu Q & A session.

Paul nodded. "How can I get access to the database?"

"You need a six-digit PIN number to access the system. But first, you need to submit an application."

"Red tape; huh?"

"Unfortunately. I will send the application to your email address. It will take about a week or two to process the request."

Paul frowned. "A week?"

"Uh…yeah, normally it takes a week."

Paul shook his head in disbelief. He worked for federal government agencies and their subsidiaries long enough to realize Barrett could have processed his application within a day if he wanted to.

"Sometimes the request takes longer," Barrett explained after he observed the Director's nonverbal response.

Paul shook his head. "No can do. I need access right away." His tone was authoritative, and his last statement was followed by a steely-eyed gaze.

"Uh…will do." Barrett was stifled by Paul's demeanor and firm tone. He glanced down and shuffled his feet, before asking, "Is there anything else I can do for you?"

Paul nodded in the affirmative. "Send me a list of pensioners and a list of new identities for spy agents and other government officials established in the past five years."

"Oh…uh…okay. But that's a lot of information. It's going to take some time for me to download the data."

"I need those lists and the application for my six-digit access code in my office. Yesterday," Paul added before leaving the computer room.

Barrett nodded in understanding. He knew what *yesterday* meant. Upon returning to his office, he slumped in his chair

54

and sulked. His Director's line of questions led him to believe that Paul was more than curious about the SCG system.

Chapter 13

Basic Instincts

When Paul returned to his office, he was more determined than ever to find out if any fraudulent activity occurred at SCG. He searched every nook and cranny in his office to see if there were any remnants of Cyrus Hampton's investigation. His efforts proved futile after searching through numerous files and cabinets.

Paul sat in his office chair to ponder the matter. Then he looked up and spotted a slightly crooked picture on the wall. He went over to straighten it, but it became detached from the screw that held it in place. Then the screw fell out of the hole.

After placing the scenic picture on the desk, he was surprised when it uncovered a small fire safe embedded in the wall. The safe had a key slot. So he searched the desk for a key, to no avail. He walked out of his office to ask his Administrative Assistant about the key to the safe, but she was not at her desk.

Undeterred, Paul went in search of tools. He ran into one of the maintenance workers, who was installing a vent in the ceiling, and asked for a screwdriver. The young man retrieved the screwdriver from his tool belt and handed it to him.

Paul thanked the maintenance worker, then returned to his office and locked the door behind him. He inserted the screwdriver in the key slot on the safe and slowly turned it counterclockwise until the lock released. Then he turned the knob on the safe and opened it.

With caution, Paul removed the contents in the safe and sat them on his desk. Then he sat in his office chair to peruse through the items, which included birth certificates, foreign and domestic passports, a marriage certificate, W-2 tax forms, and voter registration cards. He analyzed the items for several minutes before realizing there was a different name on each item.

The Select Committee for General Services was a familiar turf for Paul. He concluded the items retrieved from the safe were evidentiary documents that corresponded with the new identities and backgrounds SCG created for spy agents, military staff, and other government officials who wish to conceal their true identity. Paul was also aware that SCG created accounts for former spy agents who are eligible for retirement and wish to receive a pension based on their earnings.

He sat back in his chair, and asked, *"What is this? Are these pieces to a puzzle? None of this adds up.*

After mulling over his discovery, Paul gathered the items and put them in his briefcase. Then he grabbed the screwdriver to tighten the screw in the wall, before returning the picture to its proper place. He decided to keep the discovery of the safe and its contents to himself. Though, he believed the items might come in handy later on.

Paul returned to his desk, sat in his chair and turned on the computer monitor. He opened outlook to browse his email. Upon finding an email from the IT Team Leader, he downloaded the application for access to the SCG database. He completed the application in less than five minutes and returned it to Barrett for processing. Then he picked up the empty coffee mug from his desk before heading to the break room for a refill.

He was surprised his Administrative Assistant was at her desk. It seemed as if Sally Bates had been trying to avoid him since he reported to SCG. Regardless of her feelings for him, Paul approached her with one particular request in mind.

"I need you to obtain hard copies of Eddie Rosenthal's personnel file and have it on my desk by noon."

"Well, hello to you," she replied in a curt manner, making it clear that she was offended by his lack of courtesy.

Paul inhaled and exhaled, after checking her attitude. "Okay. Let's start over. We got off to a bad start yesterday. I can accept some responsibility for that. It's just that I did not expect so much disdain from my subordinates, especially from my Administrative Assistant."

"I'm sorry you feel that way, but I don't harbor any ill feelings toward you. I'm about business, and I always perform my job in a professional manner."

"Touché." Paul smiled and held out his hand. "I apologize for the misunderstanding."

"No apology necessary." Sally smiled and shook his hand. "I'll go to Personnel to get Eddie's file for you."

"Please keep this request confidential."

"Most certainly," Sally replied with pride in her voice. "I'll treat you no differently than I treated the former Director. I am a loyalist. You can count on me."

"I'm happy to know that," Paul said as he turned to leave. "Oh, one more thing. Please gather Cyrus Hampton's personal things in my office and mail them to his family."

"I'm on it."

"I'm going to get a cup of coffee. I'll be back shortly."

Chapter 14

Talking Heads

SCG staff members, Tameka Collins-Brown and Stephanie McPherson, headed to the breakroom after the Deputy Director met with the staff to inform them that Cyrus Hampton was murdered. They made sure no one was present as they closed the door behind them, to talk in private. Stephanie took the lead as they sat at the table furthest from the door.

"Do you know how Cyrus Hampton was murdered?" Tameka asked Stephanie in a hushed whisper.

Stephanie shrugged. "How should I know? I thought he died from a heart attack."

"This doesn't make any since. There were no news reports that indicated he was shot to death."

Stephanie rolled her eyes, before explaining, "There are other ways of murdering someone without shooting them."

"I guess you're right. You know, some people in the office are saying, 'Cyrus' body hasn't been released to the funeral home, or to his family.'"

"I'm not surprised. An autopsy is routine when a person doesn't die from natural causes. It's just a shame Cyrus died in front of his house."

Tameka's eyes widened in response. "Who told you that?"

"I have my sources," Stephanie replied with a smug grin.

Tameka dropped her head and started wringing her hands. "I just don't know...."

Stephanie rolled her eyes, figuring her friend was being dramatic as usual. "Why are you worried?"

"I'm not worried. It's just...I'm not sure why the FBI is coming to SCG to investigate Cyrus Hampton's murder. I've seen how some investigations lead to other investigations." Tameka paused, before admitting, "I have a lot on my plate. I don't want to deal with this right now."

"What do you mean?"

"It's bad enough I barely see my husband, and now I have to take care of the kids all by myself."

"Whose fault is that?"

"I'm not blaming anyone. You know my husband owns a hotel in the Virgin Islands, and it's taking up so much of his time and money."

Stephanie shook her head in disbelief. "Listen Tameka, I hear what you're saying, but it doesn't excuse the fact that his visits are becoming less frequent. It wouldn't hurt him to come home at least once a month."

"Don't do this!" Tameka banged her fist on the table and screamed in a high-pitched voice. "I don't tell you to stop spending money on your grown *ass* daughters, so don't tell me how to manage my family."

"Shush!" Stephanie held her finger to her lips as the door to the breakroom opened.

They appeared shocked when they discovered it was the SCG Director.

"Good morning, Ladies." Paul greeted them with a pleasant tone.

"Morning," Tameka mumbled while Stephanie bore a thin smile and nodded in his direction.

Paul thought these two individuals really stood out. He quickly eyed their government badges on the lanyards around their necks. Then he observed their appearance.

Stephanie was tall, bore long, blonde hair, and her eyes were ice blue. Her suit jacket exposed her cleavage, and her legs were too long for her mini skirt. Although she was smiling, Paul knew it was fake.

In contrast, Tameka was short and everything about her was Afro-centric; from her long, braided hair to her larger-than-life, gold hoop earrings. Tameka wore a black suit with a scarf made of Kente fabric. Paul thought her features closely resembled Janet Jackson, the African American pop singer.

Paul noticed the break room was eerily quiet and awkward. From the corner of his eyes, he caught the women gazing at him as he poured coffee in his mug. He surmised that he had disrupted a private conversation.

"Have a good day, Ladies," Paul said, before exiting the break room with his coffee.

"You too," they said in unison.

As soon as Paul closed the door behind him, Tameka turned to Stephanie, and asked, "Did you fuck with the new guy's car?"

"Where did you get that idea?"

"Eddie told me the Director had a flat tire in the parking lot yesterday."

Stephanie smirked. "It was just a little message."

Tameka stood up from her chair and shouted, "Why draw attention! What are you trying to prove?"

"Calm down, Tameka. You're getting bent out of shape for no reason."

Tameka folded her arms and shook her head. "Have you thought about the fact that maybe the Director was sent here because he does not scare easily?"

"Well, I don't like him."

"You're an idiot!"

"Don't call me an idiot," Stephanie retorted with vigor, before glancing at her watch. "Listen, I don't have time for this. Let's meet in the cafeteria this afternoon, to discuss further."

"Whatever," Tameka said in disgust. She abruptly left the break room, slamming the door behind her.

Stephanie was stunned by her friend's reaction. For the first time, she started to doubt Tameka's loyalty. She needed assurance that their misdeeds would remain a secret. She planned to make it clear to Tameka that she should stay the course, or she would be forced to take necessary actions to keep her in check.

Chapter 15

Eye-Opener

Paul was warmly greeted by his Administrative Assistant when he returned to his office with a fresh cup of coffee. He approached her desk, and asked, "Are there any messages for me?"

"No, Mr. Alexander. But I took care of everything you requested of me. I've already shipped Cyrus Hampton's personal items to his family, and I left Eddie Rosenthal's personnel file on your desk."

"Thank you, Sally. I appreciate your promptness. And please call me Paul."

Sally smiled. "No problem, Paul. Thank you for giving me the opportunity to clear up any misconceptions you had about me. You seem like a fine young man, and I want you to do well here at SCG. Please let me know if you need anything else."

Paul grinned and nodded before he entered his office and sat behind his desk. He was happy to have won over at least two SCG employees, Sally Bates and Eddie Rosenthal. Though, he thought his deputy's motives were questionable.

Reading through Eddie's personnel file, Paul was impressed with his outstanding military background, including his valedictorian graduate status at the Pollard Naval Institute. The service computation date showed Eddie worked for the federal government for almost thirty-five years.

Paul noted SCG was the only federal government Agency Eddie had ever worked since his honorable discharge from the Navy. Another document in the file showed he had applied for the Director's position twice before but was passed over both times.

Slouching in his chair, Paul cupped his chin after thinking there was something peculiar about Eddie's character. It was the same feeling he had about Tameka and Stephanie, the ladies he spotted in the breakroom earlier. His thoughts were interrupted when his Administrative Assistant phoned him and told him his deputy was outside his office, requesting to meet with him.

"You can send him in," he told Sally.

"Mr. Alexander," Eddie said, as he entered Paul's office.

"I prefer to be greeted on a first name basis, if you don't mind."

"Most certainly, Mr. Alexander. Sorry about that, Paul, I...um...wanted you to know that I met with the staff, and everyone is aware that the FBI may approach them with questions about Cyrus Hampton's murder."

"Good."

"Is there anything else you want me to do for you?"

"No."

Eddie stood there in silence. He was trying to think of something else to say but his mouth would not open. So many questions about Cyrus Hampton's murder was swirling around in his head. He also wanted to ask Paul about the status of the SCG investigation. However, his Director's rigid demeanor stifled his approach.

"Can…uh…Paul, can you tell me how Cyrus was murdered?"

Paul tilted his head to one side and gazed at Eddie through slanted eyes. "Why do you want to know?"

"Some of the employees were just curious, that's all."

"The toxicology report showed he was poisoned."

"Poisoned?" Eddie asked with furrowed brows.

"Yeah. Is there anything else you need to know?"

"No."

Eddie had questions about the SCG investigation, but he was afraid to venture down that path. After the men exchanged glares, Eddie bore a plastered smile before he turned around and left the office, softly closing the door behind him.

He was timid when he left his Director's office. After spotting his personnel file on Paul's desk, he could not help but wonder if he too was being investigated. Thoughts in overdrive, Eddie headed to his office, while ignoring greetings from his colleagues and subordinates along the way.

Typically, he was calm, cool, and collective. But today was different. The meeting with the Director had him on edge. He went to his office and closed the door behind him. Then he picked up the phone on his desk to call his wife.

The phone rang several times before she answered his call. Eddie shouted in the receiver, "What took you so long to answer the phone!"

"I was in the garden tending to the tomatoes. I'm afraid we might have a bad batch this year."

"Enough about the *damn* tomatoes! I need to talk to you."

Detecting anger in his voice, MaryJo gripped the phone receiver, and asked, "Honey, what's the matter?"

"You know the situation that has been going on for a while here at the job."

MaryJo knew Eddie was talking in code, so she simply asked, "Are you in trouble?"

"Not that I know of, but...." Eddie paused. He did not know what to think.

"Talk to me, Eddie. What's going on?"

"I was thinking that...maybe I should consider retiring."

"You can't do that. We have a kid in college."

"I thought about that, but I'm eligible for early retirement. I think it's best if I jump ship before things get out of control. The Acting Director might be on to me."

"Let's not be hasty. Maybe we should talk about it some more when you get home from work."

Eddie bit his bottom lip and his eyes were filled with fear. "I shouldn't have called," he thought aloud. "It's that...I have a bad feeling."

"Or you're jumping to conclusions, like you normally do."

"I suppose you're right. So sorry I bothered you. Now what were you telling me about the tomatoes?"

"Never mind. We'll talk later."

Eddie disconnected the call and chastised himself for panicking. *Why am I fretting? Paul knows nothing.* "Get it together," he said to himself. "Tie up loose ends and stay in control."

He took a deep breath and exhaled before leaving his office. Then he went to search for two women who could possibly throw a wrench in his career and freedom.

Chapter 16

Liabilities

Stephanie McPherson and Tameka Collins-Brown met in the cafeteria for lunch. Neither spoke to each other as they waited in line to pay for their salads. They sat at a table in the back of the cafeteria for privacy.

"I'm sorry for the way I talked to you earlier," Stephanie said after Tameka remained quiet. "I guess...I allowed my emotions to get in the way of common sense. I shouldn't have flattened the Director's tire."

Tameka smiled before chuckling.

"What's so funny?"

"This is the first time you've ever apologized, and you've done worse."

"Really?" Stephanie said with a mischievous grin. "What are you talking about?"

"I'd rather avoid rehashing your indiscretions. I'm more concerned about...."

Tameka stopped talking mid-sentence when she spotted Eddie approaching their table. "What does he want?" she mumbled under her breath.

"Ladies." The Deputy Director greeted them with a big smile before pulling out a chair and inviting himself to their table. "I need to talk to both of you."

Stephanie held up her hand to silence him. "We know what this is about, and now is not the time to discuss it." Her response was firm but low. She believed he wanted to ask her if she flattened the Director's tire.

"We need to be on the same page," Eddie said in a whisper. "I need both of you to keep your mouths shut when the FBI shows up."

"Why?" Tameka quizzed. "I had nothing to do with Cyrus Hampton's murder."

"That's not what I'm talking about." Eddie looked at Tameka before glancing in Stephanie's direction. "Our Director has taken it upon himself to follow through with the investigation Cyrus had initiated before he died."

Stephanie snarled. "Eddie, you told me the audit was clean."

"It was, and I'm certain the Director is not going to find what he's looking for."

"How do you know?" Stephanie asked.

"Because he's looking in the wrong place. He asked me for personnel files for SCG staff members. I even caught him browsing my file."

"Why?" Tameka asked.

"He's grasping at straws." Eddie's tone was sincere and reassuring, as he explained, "We will be fine as long as both of you refrain from establishing any more accounts. Do you understand?" he asked both of them but his eyes were glued in Stephanie's direction.

The ladies nodded in agreement. Both had three accounts each, and the accounts were generating monthly retirement income. These accounts corresponded with fake identities and backgrounds created and authorized by SCG staff who participated in the scheme.

Eddie glanced at his watch. "I have a conference call in a few minutes. We can talk later." He stood up and slid the chair under the table before leaving.

Stephanie sighed before muttering, "I don't know what I'm going to do."

Perplexed, Tameka's brow shot up. "What are you talking about?"

"I need more money."

"Why?"

"Two of the fake retirees I established have aged out and have been recently reported as deceased."

Tameka understood her friend's dilemma. The accounts they created automatically closed when the pensioner turned ninety. To resume the benefits, the pensioner must contact SCG to verify their identity and provide proof of their living status.

"We can't create any more people," Tameka explained to her friend. "You heard Eddie."

"I need you to give me money from your fake pensioners."

Tameka shook her head. "I'm sorry. I can't help you. Some of that money is tied up into my husband's hotel."

"Why are you helping him?"

"The same way you help your daughters," Tameka countered with an attitude. "They are two able-bodied individuals who refuse to get a job."

"Don't start."

"And," Tameka replied with twisted lips and a wave of her head, "don't you start with me."

Stephanie pondered her dilemma, before explaining, "I need to convince Eddie to approve the paperwork for another retiree."

"You know he won't be able to do anything as long as the new Director presides over SCG."

"I know. I wish he would get run over by a car and die." Stephanie's tone was laced with malice.

"I'm going to pretend I didn't hear that." Tameka surveyed their surroundings to make sure no one was in earshot of her friend's death-wish for their Director.

"What am I going to do, Tameka? I need money."

"Both of your daughters have Engineering degrees. It's about time they put that piece of paper to good use."

"They are working!" Stephanie snapped with rage in her eyes. "They take care of the ranch and the horses." She stood up, grabbed her purse, and turned to leave. Suddenly, she did an about face and spouted, "When you own horses, you will come to understand what it means to eat like a horse." Stephanie briskly walked out of the cafeteria, determined to get two more accounts, one way or another.

Tameka picked up her fork and resumed eating her salad. Unbothered by Stephanie's reaction, she was used to the outbursts. She hoped her friend's emotions would not cause her to do the unthinkable someday.

Chapter 17

Spin Master

It had been a long week full of problems for Paul. He was beginning to adjust to working every day, but he became irritably tired by Friday evening. When he got home, he fixed a tuna salad sandwich, opened a bottle of beer, and sat in the recliner in front of the TV to eat dinner.

Relaxing was out of the question as the events during the week wanted more re-play. Paul pondered two recent issues in his head while watching one of those talky news channels. One of the situations involved Stephanie McPherson, the SCG staff member he encountered in the breakroom on day two. He recalled that their conversation did not go over well.

"I need a new account," Stephanie had insisted, "and I need you to approve it right away."

"This request should go through the proper protocol."

"I'm aware of protocol but this is urgent. Eddie wouldn't sign off, so I'm coming to you."

"Explain the problem," Paul said as he pointed to one of the chairs on the opposite side of his desk.

Stephanie sighed as she took a seat. "Well," she began, "I have a situation where the customer is a high school Principal, but she is trying to help her mother obtain a social security number for a child who died after he was registered for school."

Paul clasped his hands with his elbows on his desk after assessing the scenario in his head. "Stephanie, isn't it true that if the child is a U.S. Citizen, a social security number was already established for him?"

"The child was born in Canada but has dual citizenship. The mother needs a social security number for insurance purposes."

"But the mother is not the customer, correct?"

"Yes, but...."

"This is not an emergency. You need to follow protocol."

Stephanie paused after analyzing Paul's demeanor. She noticed he was unyielding. "Fine!" she blurted out before walking out of his office in a huff. She was pissed after her attempt to establish a social security number for a fake pensioner was shattered.

Paul was appalled by Stephanie's behavior. He surmised she should not be helping anyone who was not an SCG customer. Further, he believed processing a social security card for a deceased applicant would raise red flags, needlessly. *Am I right or am I being too picky?* he asked himself.

Next problem. Another employee wanted to accept what he had believed a perfect ID from a customer needing a Central American background. Paul did not like the subject's name: Juan Valdez. First, it reminded him of the coffee ads. Second, it was too much like the English "John Doe." He would not like his undercover agent dealing with questions that the name might provoke, such as, *"Are you the real Juan Valdez? Or, what village are you from?"*

Paul had asked himself, "Did I make the correct decisions on these matters? They could easily be treated as no-brainers and forgotten, but deep cover stories are long term efforts."

He continued to question his competence. *Am I the new guy replacing a well-respected and seasoned Director? Are some of the situations presented to me real problems, or are they tests of my demeanor and judgement?*

Then there was the matter with his IT Team Leader, Barrett Pike. When Paul submitted his application to obtain a PIN number for access to the SCG database, Barrett told him it would be delayed because of a backlog. He asked Paul, "Did you get the printout of the new accounts, including the pensioners you requested earlier?"

"Yeah, I got them," Paul replied, after recollecting that the printout was sent to him two days after the initial request. But fifty percent of the printout contained blank space. "I still need access to the database," he persisted.

"I'm not sure why. I can get you anything you want."

Paul looked at Barrett as if he had three eyes. "Are you questioning my judgement?"

"No...no. I'm just...."

Paul said through gritted teeth, "You are to get me the access I need now. No more delays. If you can't get me what I need, I don't have a problem replacing you. Do you understand?"

"Yes. I…understand," Barrett stuttered, while sweat bullets appeared on his forehead.

Two days later, Barrett had given Paul a PIN number to access the SCG system. The problem was Paul seemed to get an error message with every click of the button. He had asked Barrett for assistance with the first five errors but gave up after realizing his lack of IT experience was to his detriment.

Overcome with fatigue, beer, and a boring news anchor, Paul closed his eyes while the lights and TV were still on. He fell asleep before he became conscious again. Two hours later, he questioned whether he was truly awake. It was eerily quiet but the beer wanting to come out made it obvious that he was not dreaming.

Paul's eyes flew open after he heard a sound that avid hikers never forget. There was a rattlesnake in his house! No two directions - two rattlesnakes. He no longer needed to go to the bathroom. Now he needed to keep his feet off the floor.

Think son. What do you do now!!!

Chapter 18

Snake Handler

Brian Jeffs was excited about the new position. He was effectively the Deputy Director of an important, little known Government Agency. The Personnel office told him to report to SCG in one week. Brian knew he would be going into a delicate situation, after Paul implied the guy with the same title may feel threatened by his presence.

Relishing the challenges that lie ahead, Brian treated himself to a baseball game in Baltimore City. One of the advantages of living in the Northeast was that it was rich in professional baseball franchises. He stopped at a pub in Fells Point after the Orioles lost to the Dodgers. Feeling friendly, he socialized with a couple of patrons and gulped a few beers.

The night was winding down, so he decided to head home. During the drive, thoughts of Maria dominated his mind and soul. He was disappointed when she had expressed her contempt for baseball or anything sports related. Brian would settle for another dinner date but getting her to commit to a second date was near impossible. She had even given him several excuses for why he could not visit her at her condo.

When Brian returned home, he tried calling Maria but there was no answer. So he took a shower and went to bed.

The ringing phone woke him after he fell into a deep sleep. The caller ID showed it was Paul calling, and not his needy brother this time. "What's up?" he answered the phone in a muffled voice.

"Brian, I'm in trouble," Paul shakily admitted. "I need you to come over with your snake gear. My house is dark. My cell phone is at seven percent so I will need to power it off soon."

Alarmed by Paul's frantic tone, Brian rose out of bed and turned on the lamp. "You're in trouble," he paraphrased in a slow tone, "and you need me to bring snake gear at three o'clock in the morning. What am I missing here?"

Sweating bullets, Paul said in a methodical and slow tone, "I will give you a better explanation if you can rescue me. I'm in my recliner, in a totally dark house. I hear rattlesnakes," he whispered after being spooked by the hissing sounds. "Help, please. I also need to go to the bathroom with a sense of urgency. Can you get over here quickly? It would be bad for an adult to pee on the living room furniture."

It seemed like forever, but Brian got over there and found Paul's house in total darkness. The moon was behind a cloud, so the outside was as pitch black as the inside. Using a camper lantern, Brian found the main breaker. It was OFF. He flipped it back on and the lights illuminated the inside of the house.

Brian did a circuit of the perimeter and found nothing amiss. He knocked on the front door, but there was no answer. Then he retrieved his cell phone from his back pocket to call Paul.

"Thanks buddy," Paul said with relief. "I didn't see the damn snakes when the lights turned on, so I'm in the bathroom. I will be at the front door in a sec."

"Okay. I will go around the house to check the windows and doors. I'll meet you out front."

Brian checked the backyard and all seemed secure. By the time he got to the front door, Paul stepped outside and greeted his friend with a handshake.

"Have I thanked you for coming so quickly? Thank you and thank you. I didn't see snakes inside, and I no longer hear them. Where in the *hell* could they have gone?"

Brian shrugged. "Not out of the windows or doors. The outside of your house is secure. Let me check inside the house, just in case."

Paul stepped aside for Brian to enter his home. "Do your snake thing carefully, while I try to keep my feet off the floor." He sat on his recliner and pushed the lever on the side of the chair, to flip the leg rest up.

Walking throughout the house with his snake equipment, Brian searched every room, nook and cranny. It took only a few minutes for him to figure out there was not even one snake in the house. He trusted that his friend was not imagining things, especially after all the hiking and camping they had done.

Cupping his chin, Brian thought aloud, "Two rattlesnakes did not climb the wall, open the windows and screens, and crawl out. The doors were built for Maryland winters, so they did not go under the door."

"That's what I was thinking," Paul countered.

"Why don't we turn off the lights and listen for the snakes?"

"Good idea."

Paul turned off the lights in the kitchen and bedroom, and Brian turned off the lights in the den. Then they sat in the darkness. After a few minutes of quiet, their ears perked up and their eyes widened. They heard the rattle snakes coming from two directions.

"They are in the same two locations as before," Paul said with certainty. "I think that's strange. Since I'm your new boss and you came to help me, I'm remaining on the recliner while you turn on the lights."

Brian chuckled. "You're a coward, but I'll do it." He walked over and flipped on the light switch. "I don't see any snakes."

"I'm happy you heard them. So, I'm a coward, but not a total idiot."

Brian snickered. "I never doubted you. Let's rest and check outside when it's daylight."

"We can stay in the living room," Paul suggested before returning to the recliner.

Brian removed his jacket and stretched out on the sofa across from his friend. They were comfortable in each other's presence, so they did not have to talk. They relaxed until daybreak. At some point, they needed to figure out the 'who' and 'why' regarding the snake sounds.

Chapter 19

Loose Cannon

Earlier, Stephanie and her daughter, Becky, had parked their car a quarter of a mile from Paul Alexander's home, which was in a secluded and heavily wooded area. They sat in the dark for hours waiting for Paul to run out of his home once he heard the snake sounds.

"I don't see why we have to be here, to witness this," Becky complained.

"Don't do this," Stephanie warned through slanted eyes and gritted teeth.

"What do you expect to happen?"

"I'm not sure." Stephanie's tone was somber as she pondered her eldest daughter's question.

"Okay, Mom. What is the objective?"

"To make him go away," Stephanie snapped. She was agitated because she did not think through her plan, and her daughter was asking valid questions. "I figure I would make him paranoid and force him to resign from SCG."

Becky stared at her mother in disbelief. She could not believe her mother didn't think through her plan.

Stephanie felt her daughter's gaze from the corner of her eye. Exasperated, she turned to her daughter, and asked, "Do you like the lifestyle I'm able to provide for you and your sister? The farm and the horses? You know how much money is needed to maintain our standard of living?"

"Yeah, but…."

"Listen to me!" Stephanie barked while shooting daggers at her daughter. "I work hard for SCG, and I'm not going to sit by and let this Paul guy interfere with my plans. We deserve everything *we* have."

Becky nodded in understanding. She decided not to argue with her mother, because forcing her to listen to reason was pointless. Though, Becky had a feeling her mother's actions against the Director would come back to haunt them one day.

At age fifty, Stephanie never imagined owning a farm would be so expensive. She also never thought she would be divorced from her husband after twenty-five years of marriage. She was shocked when he left her and their children without an explanation or warning. They never heard from him again. Stephanie was angry but her daughters were saddened by his departure.

To fill the void in their lives, and in hers, Stephanie bought a small farm in Adamstown, Maryland, a municipality of Fredrick County. Attached to the farm was a four-bedroom rancher that needed a few updates. The idea made sense because she and the girls loved horses and loved living off the grid.

The farm was already established by a previous owner who fell ill and was not able to oversee the day-to-day operations. Transferring ownership of the farm was the easy part but working on the farm was not what Stephanie had expected. She soon learned that caring for and feeding horses, cattle, chickens, and pigs was overwhelming and financially burdensome.

Stephanie and her daughters provided horse riding lessons and offered stable boarding to pay the small staff and offset some of the farming expenses. It was not enough. They were in the hole and risked losing the farm and their home.

"Who is that?" Becky asked, after she noticed headlights coming from behind their parked car. She looked in the side view mirror to get a better view of the driver, but the oncoming headlights blurred her vision.

"I don't know," Stephanie replied, after she spotted the headlights. "Let's duck down, so no one will see us."

A few seconds later, they sat up in their car seat and noticed the car was headed to Paul's house. They became alarmed when Paul's visitor climbed out of the car and rushed toward the front door.

"What are we going to do now?" Becky asked her mother. "It seems your boss has company."

"Yeah, I know."

"Let's get out of here. We'll think of something else." Stephanie started the ignition, made a U-turn, and headed home. With the arrival of the unexpected visitor, she believed her plans to scare her Director may have failed.

Since day one, Stephanie had been following Paul Alexander to find out where he lived, the places he frequented and tidbits about everyone in his orbit. Her colleague had told her the make and model of the Director's car on his first day of work.

Stephanie had gone to the garage after lunch to look for his car. Then she knelt down by the rear tire on the driver's side to deflate the tire by removing the valve stem cap and inserting the pointy part of an ink pen. Satisfied with the results, Stephanie returned to work and pretended as if nothing happened. She had hoped her actions would have been enough to make Paul think twice about working for SCG.

In deep thought, she mulled over her next ploy to get rid of Paul while Becky slept during the hour-long drive to Adamstown, Maryland. She looked over at her daughter who was sound asleep. Smiling with a wicked grin, she acknowledged her daughter had inherited her good looks, blue eyes, slim waist, and curvy physique.

We can pull this off, Stephanie thought to herself. Every man was attracted to boobs and butts. Stephanie figured the essence of a sexy woman, like her daughter, could be Paul's weakness. Nodding and smirking, pieces of her plan were coming together. She made a mental note to stop by the mall and do some shopping in preparation for the next big plan.

Chapter 20

Stranger Things

As daylight broke, Brian rolled over on the sofa and turned toward Paul, who was laid back in the recliner. He noticed his friend was facing the ceiling but could not tell if his eyes were open. He lifted his head, and asked, "Are you up?"

"Yeah," Paul mumbled. "I couldn't sleep."

"I told you I didn't find any snakes."

Paul sighed before turning to his friend. "It's not that. It's just some strange things have been happening since I started working at SCG."

"Such as?"

"On day one, I had a flat tire in a well-guarded parking lot."

Brian frowned. "Did someone put a hole in your tire?"

Paul shook his head. "No, Triple A did not find any holes so they used an air pump to inflate my tire."

"Maybe it was a slow leak."

"You're probably right." Paul refrained from telling Brian that his staff, including the Deputy Director, were acting strange in his presence. He also did not mention that the IT

Team Leader may have made it difficult for him to access the SCG database.

Brian detected that his friend was worried, and possibly scared. He wanted to do something to put Paul's mind at ease. So he suggested that they search the house again. "We need to make sure you have a snake-free house," he added with a slight chuckle.

Peeling themselves off the sofa and recliner, they moved at a slow and careful pace while scanning every room in the house. Nothing was out of the ordinary, so they started to relax.

They froze in place after they heard the sound again. Then they checked the windows and doors again and again, but they were all secure.

Brian said, "It's time to explore outside. I suggest we do it together."

While outside in the front yard, Paul said, "That's the biggest moth I've ever seen." He looked at the moth on the window and saw a thin wire dangling from it. Then he noticed a moth on every window on that side of the house. "I got something!" he shouted out to Brian, as he removed the moth with the dangling wires.

Brian ran over to Paul and frowned at what resembled a moth. "What is that?"

Paul placed his index finger to his lips. Then he held it up so his friend could see the dangling wires between his fingers.

Brian nodded in understanding, after inspecting the wires affixed to the fake moth were little transmitters.

They remained quiet while strategically removing the fake moth and transmitters from the windows. Then they turned them off and placed them in a box Paul had retrieved from his coat closet.

"It's been a successful morning of snake hunting," Brian joked, after Paul put the box of transmitters in the coat closet.

"I know," Paul chuckled, but the discovery of the transmitters had him on edge.

"Do you know who would go through the trouble of installing the transmitters?"

"I'm not sure but I think it may be related to my mere presence at SCG."

"You are one of the smartest guys I know. If anyone can find the culprit, I'll place my bet on you."

"I appreciate the vote of confidence."

Brian sniggered when a loud sound growled from his stomach. "I think that grumbling sound means I'm hungry. Are there any good places for breakfast in this little town?"

"You don't have to go anywhere. I'll cook you some breakfast."

"Sounds good to me."

***

Over breakfast, Paul told Brian about the two incidents at work, the quirkiness of some of the staff, and other problems he could foresee.

Brian nodded. "And let's not forget the transmitters we just discovered around your house."

"I know. Someone is trying to scare the *hell* out of me."

"Is it working?"

Paul smirked. "You damn *Skippy*!"

"Is it enough to make you reconsider the job?"

"Hell no! I'm determined now more than ever to find out what the hell is going on." Paul turned to his friend with a look of concern. "Are you reconsidering the job offer as my deputy?"

"Not me," Brian boasted. "I'll be with you every step of the way."

"I appreciate that. How do you feel about leaving your job at the Department of Defense?"

"No love lost there. This new job is exactly what I needed."

"Remember, I told you my tenure at SCG is temporary."

"Yeah, I know. But I look forward to a new beginning. The Personnel office told me I can report to SCG in a week."

"That's good to hear. I look forward to working with you."

"Me too."

"How's your brother?"

"Don't ask. He thinks I'm his personal ATM."

Paul burst out laughing. "You started this mess with your brother, and you can finish it."

"I know."

"Now let's focus on a serious matter. Are you dating anyone?"

Brian grinned. "Yeah. Her name is Maria. She's a colleague."

"Based on that silly grin on your face, it sounds like it could be serious."

"I hope so."

"It's about time you started dating someone, other than the nutcases you've dated in the past."

"Please don't bring that up."

Brian could not forget how he had spent three years dating his ex-girlfriend. He had waited for the right moment to propose to her in front of their family and friends. It was supposed to be an engagement celebration, but it ended up being a break-up party. He was crushed when she coldly told him, *"No, I can never marry anyone like you. You have absolutely ruined a wonderful friendship-and it had benefits!"*

Head hung low, Brian had left the party and went into hiding for two weeks. That was the last time he saw his ex-girlfriend. He had gone out of his way to avoid all communication with her.

90

"Life happens," Paul said in a comforting tone. "I learned to take the good with the bad and keep it moving."

"Ditto."

"So, do you think there's a chance I'm going to meet your new lady friend?"

"Yeah, I think so."

Brian had been thinking about Maria ever since their first and only date. He believed he was in-love with her. Though, he was not sure if her feelings for him were mutual. He checked his watch before gulping down a glass of orange juice. "I gotta leave now. I have a lot of errands to run. What do you have planned this morning?"

"No plans yet. I'm just going to review some case files from the office and try to relax the rest of the day. At least I don't have to worry about those invisible snakes."

Brian chuckled as he stood up to leave. He noticed Paul's newly charged cell phone began to ring, which was followed by a popular song.

Paul interrupted the call by hitting the 'Do Not Disturb' option, which forced the call to voicemail. Then he turned his attention to Brian, "I appreciate your coming so quickly. You are a lifesaver."

"No problem. I'll chat with you later."

"Thanks again, for coming to my rescue."

Chapter 21

Battle of the Egos

Paul was enjoying his conversation with Brian over breakfast when he heard Lionel Ritchie's famous "Hello" song blaring from his cell phone. He had programmed his cell to play that song every time Liz called. Decidedly, he allowed her call to go to voicemail. He was not ready for his friend to know about his relationship with the President of the United States.

After Brian left his home, he cleaned the kitchen and washed the dishes. Then he sat on the stool at the breakfast nook and returned Liz's call. He frowned when he heard a familiar voice.

"Why are you answering her phone?" His question was terse and firm.

Jimmy Johnson, the President's Senior Advisor, smirked in response. "Liz is taking her morning ablution, so I have been enlisted to answer her calls."

"Can you use words we commoners understand?"

Sighing, Jimmy explained, "She went for a jog, and now she's washing the sweat away before her briefings with the Executive staff."

"I'll call back."

"Don't hang up. I will transfer your call to the Secret Service Agent who is protecting her. Hold on for a second."

A brief time later, Liz was on her Agent's phone. She sounded breathless but energized from her two-mile run. "Hi, Paul. So, you don't answer my calls anymore? I am certain it was breakfast time, or maybe you were entertaining a special person."

Paul smiled. "Actually, Brian Jeffs was here. He just left."

"Your new deputy?"

"Yes."

Liz chuckled. "Did he sleep over?"

"Jealous, are we?" Paul teased. "Did you forget about the lady with the small boobs and big butt already?"

"Touché. What prompted your friend's visit?"

"In the middle of the morning, I awoke to the sound of rattlesnakes in a dark house. I panicked at the thought of reptiles devouring my body. I called Brian for help."

"Are you serious?" Liz asked with shock and awe in her voice.

"Fortunately, Brian is good with snakes. He came to my rescue."

"I presume he killed them before they bit you or gave you a heart attack."

"No snakes were found. But we found transmitters disguised as a moth. I need to have them analyzed."

"Mail them to the drop. Jimmy will get them checked for you. Anything else?" Liz asked, without skipping a beat.

Paul hesitated before answering her question. He did not want to bother Liz with some of the oddities at work so he kept it simple. "Work seems okay. The people seem okay. My current deputy, Eddie, appears not to be happy to have me around. I can't put my finger on it, but there's something strange about him."

"Why do you feel that way?"

"I'm not sure, but I'm certain he's hiding some resentment for not getting the director's job."

"I understand what you're saying. What can I do to put his mind at ease?"

"Nothing, I suppose, especially since Cyrus Hampton's murder hasn't been solved and the SCG investigation is in full force."

Liz nodded. "I guess you're right. Do you have any leads on the SCG probe?"

Paul shook his head. "Not yet. I hope to have more insight about the staff soon. I'll keep you posted."

"I'd appreciate that. Take care, my love."

"You too."

Paul had refrained from telling Liz about the safe in his office and its contents. He needed more time to explore whether the items were a part of the SCG investigation that was initiated by the former Director.

Chapter 22

Pressure Cooker

HR Team Leader, Tameka Collins-Brown questioned whether her criminal actions at the Select Committee for General Services were worth it. When her now deceased Director, Cyrus Hampton, approached her two days before he was murdered, Tameka became concerned he had discovered she was involved with embezzling funds from the SCG.

"Are you sure you don't have anything to tell me?" he had asked Tameka when they met in his office.

"Yes, I'm sure," her voice quivered. "Why do you ask?"

Cyrus sighed before he stood up, crossed his arms, and stared down at her with a knowing gaze. "I'll give you time to think about whether you want to come clean. But keep this in mind - your children will suffer if you go to jail for committing fraud."

"I...I...." Stuttering and staggering, Tameka found it difficult to respond. "I need time....to think about this."

"You have until this weekend to come clean. When the flood gates open, you will be on your own and I won't be able to help you."

"I understand." Tameka dropped her head in despair before she stood up to leave. The first thing she did was tell Stephanie and her Deputy Director about the conversation she had with Cyrus.

"What did he say, specifically?" Eddie pried, hoping Tameka did not spill the beans.

"He didn't mention any specifics."

"I think he's bluffing," Stephanie interjected.

Tameka shook her head. "But…we don't know for sure what he knows."

"But I do." Eddie stood in front of Tameka and peered into her eyes. "What did you tell him?"

"Nothing."

"Good," Eddie said with a nod, "and keep it that way."

"But…but you don't understand. Cyrus told me the flood gates will open on Monday."

"What does that mean?" Stephanie asked, eyeing Tameka with suspicion.

"Nothing," Eddie said with confidence. "He's pulling your leg."

Tameka did not feel comforted by Eddie's assurance. Prior to Cyrus Hampton's death, she had already made up her mind to tell him everything she knew, including her role in the pension scheme. She was alarmed when she found out he was murdered.

Both Stephanie and Tameka had ironclad alibis the night Cyrus was murdered. They were together in Washington, DC, watching a musical at the Lincoln Hall. Though, Tameka could not help but wonder if Stephanie was involved with Cyrus's demise.

***

At the present, Tameka had not spoken with Stephanie since their last encounter in the cafeteria. She believed Stephanie was reckless and could implicate her in embezzling funds from SCG. She was shocked when Stephanie sent her text messages asking her to establish two more accounts for fake pensioners. Tameka blocked her colleague's phone number, hoping to send a message.

But Stephanie was relentless. She stormed into the HR office to confront her friend. Then she sat in the empty chair next to Tameka's desk and waited for her to report to work.

When Tameka walked in her office, she was not happy to see the one person she had been trying to avoid. She stared at Stephanie as she placed her handbag in her bottom drawer and sat in her chair.

"What can I do for you, Stephanie?"

"I tried calling but evidently you blocked my number. I just need to know did you establish the new accounts."

"I thought about it, but only for a second. I can't, and I won't do it." Crossing her arms, Tameka's response was firm and unyielding.

Stephanie was unnerved by her friend's response. She stood up and faced Tameka with a crooked smile and snooty attitude. Her words were choppy, as she said, "Oh... yes... you...will."

Unfazed, Tameka uncrossed her arms, sat back in her chair, and twisted her lips. She stared at Stephanie through slanted eyes, before asking, "What are you going to do if I don't?"

"Do you really want to be in a situation to find out?"

Tameka took a deep breath an exhaled.

"I didn't think so," Stephanie responded with a flip of her hair.

"Let me get this right. You want me to do this for you, even though Eddie told both of us not to create any more accounts, the FBI is investigating Cyrus Hampton's murder, and the new Director reignited the SCG investigation?"

"Yes I do." Stephanie pursed her lips and crossed her arms to show she was serious.

"Are you crazy? We can go to jail for this."

"Not if you keep your big mouth shut. Create two more pensioners for me. I expect the first check in two weeks…or else."

Suddenly, Tameka was shaken by Stephanie's threat. "You know…uh…things don't happen that fast."

"You have access to discretionary funds for emergency payments. Use them!" Stephanie screamed, before she turned around and stormed out of Tameka's office.

"That bitch," an exasperated Tameka mouthed. She needed a way out of this matter but did not know who to trust. Doing nothing was not an option.

Chapter 23

Spooked

After mailing the transmitters to the drop box at the White House, Paul returned to work to focus on the Select Committee for General Services' investigation. He was more determined now than ever to find out what his predecessor knew before he was murdered. Getting spooked by rattle snake sounds over the weekend only ignited his desire to continue with the SCG probe.

He resumed reviewing the files his deputy had delivered last week. Tameka Collins-Brown's personnel folder had piqued his interest. Paul realized she supplied the first signature for new pensioners created by the SCG staff. The SCG Director or the Deputy typically supplied the second signature.

He picked up the phone on his desk and called his Administrative Assistant. "Sally, please arrange for Tameka Collins-Brown to report to my office in an hour."

"Will do. Do you need anything else?"

"No, that'll be all for now."

"Hold on, Paul," Sally said after she looked up and noticed the Deputy Director standing in front of her desk. "Hello Eddie, how can I help you?"

"Is the Director available?"

"Send him in," Paul said after hearing the exchange over the phone.

Sally turned to Eddie. "You can go in his office."

"Thanks Sally."

"Good morning," Eddie said as he entered Paul's office with a file in his hand. His tone was upbeat but forced.

"Morning. What can I do for you?"

"One of my writers told me you questioned one of the products I approved." Eddie handed the file to Paul with the business proposal for the project in question.

Paul took a second to review the file, then handed it back to Eddie. "It was shoddy work."

"I understand your perception," Eddie explained. "But, in my opinion, this product is good and ready to be published."

"It needs more work. How long will it take you to review the product, and make the necessary changes?"

Biting his tongue, Eddie asked, "Can I say something?"

"Sure."

"I've been employed here for a long time. I happen to know what passes mustard around here."

"Eddie, I appreciate your experience, but I'm your boss and I'll be the judge of what passes mustard. Again, how long is it going to take for you to review this product, and bring it up to par?"

"Give me a couple of weeks."

"You have one week. You can leave now."

Paul shook his head after Eddie left his office. All the niceties Eddie had displayed in the beginning was just a façade. Though, he had to admit his deputy's expertise was invaluable. Finding a way to blend their egos was possible but Eddie's cooperation with the SCG investigation was a different story.

***

Turning on his heels, Eddie left Paul's office sizzling with internal rage. He returned to his office, threw the file on his desk, and shouted, "What a jerk! This product is perfectly fine the way it is."

"What's going on?" Stephanie asked, after walking into Eddie's office, and noticing the scowl on his face.

"Nothing."

"Are you sure?"

"Yeah. I just have to keep my cool with the new boss. Did you need anything?" Eddie asked after Stephanie sat in the chair across from his desk.

"Uh…yeah. Did you know the Director had just arranged a meeting with Tameka?"

"He did?" Eddie's right eyebrow shot up.

"So you didn't know." Stephanie blew out air in a huff. "I don't know about you, but this Paul guy is getting on my nerves."

She was upset because her latest tactics did not convince Paul to quit the job as the SCG Director. Luckily, she and her daughter wore gloves when they planted the transmitters outside his home. Her mind was racing to think of another ploy to torment her enemy.

Eddie looked up at his partner-in-crime through slanted eyes. "Stephanie," he said in a calm voice, "Whatever you do, don't do anything crazy. We need level heads around here to deal with someone like Paul Alexander."

"I know," Stephanie nodded. She and her daughter had gone through the trouble of scaring the Director, but their efforts appeared to have failed. Unyielding, she was working on Plan B, to make sure Paul became a figment of her imagination.

"Don't worry, Eddie,' she said with assurance. "I'll take care of him."

"No you won't," Eddie snapped.

"But…."

"I don't want you to do anything that will bring attention to SCG."

"Okay, whatever." Stephanie took a deep breath and exhaled, before walking out of Eddie's office.

Squinting his eyes, Eddie had a sneaky feeling Stephanie was up to something. He hoped she did not do anything that affected his chances of getting a promotion, even though he had a feeling his chances had greatly diminished.

"Geez," Eddie whispered when the FBI appeared in his office door entry. "What now?"

"May we come in?" the agent asked. "We'd like to ask you some questions involving Cyrus Hampton's murder."

An exasperated Eddie thought, *Do I have a choice?* A realistic Eddie said, "Certainly, how can I help you guys?"

Chapter 24

Déjà vu

When Tameka walked into Paul's office, he was seated behind his desk looking at a file. She looked closer and noticed her name on some of the contents in the folder. "Mr. Alexander, you asked to meet with me."

"You can call me Paul. Have a seat," he said, as he pointed to the vacant chair across from his desk.

Tameka stood in the door entry for a few seconds before obliging his request.

"I've been looking at your file," Paul said after Tameka sat down, "and noticed you've been with SCG for ten years. You have an impressive performance record."

"Thank you." Tameka's voice was soft and timid.

"I also noticed you have a high-level of security access to SCG data."

"Well...I can explain. Um...I pre-approve most of the accounts established for SCG. But the Director and Deputy Director provides the final signoff."

Paul nodded. "That's great. That piece of information lets me know you're the right person I should be speaking with."

"What do you mean?"

Paul crossed his arms, placed his elbows on his desk, and leaned toward Tameka before asking, "Were you in communication with the SCG Director before he died?"

Tameka clasped her hands in her laps and began wringing them. She did not know what to say. *Should I tell him the truth, or should I lie?*

"Well?" Paul persisted.

"We communicated often."

Paul frowned. "Cyrus Hampton was investigating potential fraud here at SCG. Do you know if the investigation had anything to do with his murder?"

Tameka shrugged. "I don't know."

Paul did not respond as he unfolded his arms and sat back in his chair. He looked into Tameka's eyes and sensed fear. It was a wild guess, but he believed she knew more than she let on. "Do you have children?"

Tameka nodded.

"I'll give you time to think about whether you want to come clean. But keep this in mind - your children will suffer if you go to jail for committing fraud."

Paul stopped talking long enough for Tameka to digest what he was saying. He noticed the worry lines on her forehead when she casted her eyes downward. "Mrs. Brown, you need to decide what is in the best interest for your family. When the flood gates open, you will be on your own and I won't be able to help you."

Tameka's eyes flew open in response. *Oh my God! Cyrus Hampton told me the same thing before he was murdered.* She felt uncomfortable at the way Paul glared at her. She stood up to leave, after asking, "Is there anything else you need from me?"

"I'll be here when you are ready to talk. You can also reach me on my cell phone." He jotted his cell number on a note page and handed it to her.

"Thank you," Tameka mumbled as she took the note page from him. Then she turned around to leave his office.

Paul pondered whether his bluff would backfire. He was not even sure if any criminal activity had occurred at SCG. To thwart any opportunities to commit fraud, Paul phoned Eddie and told him that he would give the final approval for all new pensioners.

"But that's my job," Eddie resisted with bass in his voice.

Paul ignored Eddie's snappy tone. "Feel free to continue reviewing the requests, but I will have the final say on whether new pensioners will be approved. Do you understand?"

The blood seemed to drain from Eddie's face at the realization that his power at SCG was waning. He wanted to say something, anything to let Paul know where he stood. Lacking courage, Eddie simply said, "Yes, I understand."

***

When Tameka left the Director's office, she believed he suspected she was a part of the scheme to defraud the government. She needed to talk to her co-worker, Stephanie,

106

about her conversation with Paul, but she had to pick up her husband from the airport in an hour.

So she returned to her desk to submit an electronic leave slip for the remainder of the day. Then she submitted another leave slip to take off the next day to spend time with her family. Pressed for time, she hurriedly grabbed her purse and car keys before exiting the building.

During the drive to the airport, Tameka reminisced on how she got involved with defrauding the government. Her colleagues had approached her at a time when she was vulnerable. She and her family had lived a simpler life in a three-bedroom, two-bath stucco in Washington DC. The home was in a rough area but the mortgage was affordable. The problem was that her husband could not keep a job, and they fell behind in paying their bills. Also, their children were enrolled in a public school that had a bad reputation.

Tameka decided early on that the money she received from the fake pensioners would only be for a short period. She had used the money to purchase a bigger house for her family in a safe community in Alexandria, Virginia. Then she enrolled her seven-year-old son and ten-year-old twin daughters in private school and paid off outstanding debts.

Life was stable until her husband got the bright idea to buy and run a hotel in the Virgin Islands. Expenses related to the hotel had forced her to be financially dependent on the money from the fake pensioners, for a much longer period than she had anticipated. Now she was left to think about the repercussions of her actions.

Chapter 25

Good vs Evil

Brian was disappointed after his girlfriend, Maria Hernandez, turned down his invitation to go on a walking trail in the Harpers Ferry National Park. The park stretched along the borders of West Virginia, Washington, DC, and Maryland. He thought it would have been a good opportunity to get to know her better.

"I'm sorry," Maria said with sadness in her voice. "I'm just not in the mood for walking."

"Well, how about a picnic at the National Mall in DC?"

"It's sounds nice but...um...one sec."

Placing her ear to the door, Maria wanted to make sure her supervisor, who was the Chief Officer at the Department of Defense, was not eavesdropping on her conversation with Brian. Her supervisor had paid her an unexpected visit earlier, and she knew he would be enraged if he discovered another man was interested in her.

Breathing a sigh of relief, Maria calmed down after hearing her supervisor on his cell phone discussing a business transaction.

"Brian," she resumed the conversation in a hushed whisper, "can I call you back?"

"Sure."

Maria disconnected the phone, opened the bathroom door, and stood eye-to-eye with her supervisor.

"Who were you speaking with on the phone?" he asked with daggers in his eyes. When she did not answer him right away, he started barging toward her.

Fearful that he might hurt her, Maria took a step back and her cell phone slipped from her hand and onto the floor. "Uh...no one," she finally said after she could not think of a good lie.

"Don't lie to me!"

"Why do you care?"

"Don't get indignant with me. I gave you that promotion, and I can take it from you."

Maria's eyes began to water. "Why are you doing this?"

"I'm making sure you understand that loyalty goes both ways."

"This is getting old," Maria sniffled through tears. "You don't own me. Besides, I've been dating someone special."

Her supervisor glared and twisted his lips from anger. "When did this happen?"

"The same day you told me I was promoted as your Branch Chief."

"So you used me?"

"We used each other. You are married," Maria said with force. Then she crossed her arms and leaned on one leg, before spouting, "I wonder how your wife would feel if she knew her husband was screwing his subordinate."

The Chief Officer shook his head, finding it hard to believe what he was hearing. Maria had always been submissive to him. He wondered what changed. He took a step back from her, then brushed his hand over his head in frustration.

Pacing back and forth, he felt fearful of his wife finding out about the affair. *She would take everything in the divorce,* he thought to himself. *And Maria, after all I've done for her, now she's stabbing me in the back.*

The Chief Officer stopped in his tracks and turned toward Maria, before asking, "Who is he?"

"I don't want to say."

"Is it someone I know?"

Maria did not respond as she casted her eyes to the floor.

"Does he work for the Department of Defense?"

Maria continued to remain mum.

Suddenly, the Chief Officer's eyes widened as if he had an epiphany. It dawned on him that Maria's promotion coincided with Brian Jeffs' promotion to another government agency. His tone was filled with rage when he finally spoke. "You told me you started dating someone the same day I promoted you."

Maria nodded in the affirmative.

"Is it Brian Jeffs?"

Maria's mouth flew open in response to his question. Suddenly, she became protective of Brian. She did not want anything to happen to him.

"Your nonresponse tells me everything I need to know. I'm going to take care of Jeffs," he said in a menacing tone, "then I'll take care of you later." The Chief Officer rushed toward her front door.

"Wait!" Maria hollered out. "What are you going to do? Are you going to hurt him?"

Her supervisor grabbed the doorknob to the front door before turning back to her. "I'm going to kill him."

"Is it worth it? You are going to throw your career and family away. And for what? Over an affair?"

Maria's questions struck a nerve. He dropped his head in shame. "You are right," he admitted after deep thought. "I'm sorry I ever got involved with you. You and I are done."

"Wait, what about my promotion?"

"You blew it! I will arrange for your transfer to another department ASAP!" On that note, the Chief Officer walked out of Maria's condo and never looked back to see her crying and falling to the floor.

After drowning in tears, Maria gathered her body off the floor to put things in perspective. She was sad and happy at the same time. She was happy over the prospect of getting her supervisor out of her bed for good. Though, she was sad because she jeopardized the promotion she always wanted.

In retrospect, it dawned on Maria that having a relationship with Brian could be healthy for her heart and soul.

For the first time ever, she believed she found someone to love her without expecting anything in return.

Maria wiped away her tears with the back of her hand as she stood and retrieved her cell phone from the floor. Then she called Brian to tell him she wanted to go to the National Mall and have a picnic. She was ready to commit to a new beginning.

***

Brian was surprised but elated Maria had agreed to the picnic outing, where they shared a bottle of wine and fed each other grapes and strawberries. Then they walked a short trail admiring the scenery.

At one point, Brian stopped to stare into her eyes, which made her blush. "I like you Maria," he admitted with dreamy eyes. "I've always liked you. I wish moments like this never ended."

"It doesn't have to." Maria stepped closer to Brian and kissed him on the lips while inserting her tongue. Then she looked down and noticed the bulge in his pants. "You want to come over to my condo to take care of that?"

Brian chuckled. "I would love to but I don't want to rush things between us. I want to learn everything about you, because I want you to be a part of my life."

Maria's mouth flew open in response. "Are you saying what I think you're saying."

"Yes, I hope you will be my wife someday."

She took a deep breath and exhaled.

"Don't worry," Brian said with a slight chuckle. "I don't plan on proposing today. I just wanted you to know my intentions." He grabbed her hand and kissed her on the forehead. "Let's get out of here. We have to go to work tomorrow. But maybe we can do something special this weekend."

Maria smiled. "I'd like that."

Chapter 26

Trouble in Paradise

Forty-five minutes later, Tameka arrived at the airport in record time. She parked her car on the second floor in the BWI parking garage near the airport entrance, as per her husband's instructions. Then she reclined in her seat and closed her eyes. Distraught and tired, Tameka was overwhelmed at the thought of not being able to raise her kids if she was locked up for committing fraud.

"A penny for your thoughts," her husband, Andy, said after he walked around to the driver's side of her car and kissed her on the cheek.

Tameka turned to her husband in surprise. "Uh...Andy...I didn't know your plane had already landed."

"The plane arrived a few minutes early. I tried calling you."

Tameka retrieved her cell phone from her purse to review her phone history. She frowned, after explaining, "There are no missed calls from you."

Andy shrugged. "Must've been a bad connection. Pop the trunk." He stowed his suitcase in the trunk after it flew open. Then he climbed in the passenger seat, plugged his cell phone in the car charger, and buckled his seatbelt.

Tameka asked, "Do you want to drive?"

"Nah. You can handle it. Besides, I have to make some phone calls to make sure the hotel is running smoothly in my absence."

He reached for his cell phone on the console, but Tameka grabbed it first. "No phone calls. We need to talk about the hotel."

Andy snatched his phone from her. "What is wrong with you?"

"I told you, we need to talk."

"Talk about what?"

Tameka sighed before responding. "I'm tired of raising the kids by myself. I was thinking, maybe we can find a hotel in Maryland or DC you can invest in."

"We talked about this before. I need to make enough money to take care of my family."

"But that's the problem. You're not taking care of your family, I am."

Andy grimaced. "What are you saying?"

"You're hardly ever home. Our kids need their father."

"It was not my idea to have three kids in the first place," Andy replied with an attitude. "Listen, I didn't fly home for you to nag me. I don't need this *shit* from you."

"And I don't want to argue with you."

"So let's not." Andy made clear the conversation with his wife was over as he phoned his hotel in the Virgin Islands. In response, Tameka blew out air in frustration before she pulled out of the parking space and exited the parking garage.

Andy spent a couple of minutes on the phone before giggling like a little schoolboy. Toward the end of the call, he smiled and said, "Me too."

Tameka's eyes and ears instantly perked up. *What the hell? That's what he says to me when I tell him 'I love him' over the phone. Who is he talking to?*

"I'll call you later," Andy cooed in the receiver before disconnecting the call. Then he reclined in the passenger seat with a big grin on his face.

"Who was that on the phone?"

Andy hesitated before answering her. "My new manager." The lie slipped from his lips with ease. Actually, the person on the phone was a former beauty queen he had hired as the main attraction to his hotel. The sexual favors she gave him were a bonus.

"When did you get a new manager?" Tameka asked with raised brows.

Andy blew out air, feigning annoyance. "Do I have to tell you everything? All you should be concerned with is making sure we have enough money to renovate *my* hotel."

"Your hotel?" Tameka glanced at her husband in disgust.

"You know what I mean."

Tameka was livid. She did not know what was more pressing, the woman she suspected on the phone with her husband or their money problems. She chose the latter. She took a deep breath to calm herself, before commenting, "I deposit sufficient funds in the business account every month for the renovations, but I haven't received a return on our investment. I know, for a fact, that the hotel is booked all the time."

"But do you know the costs of the renovations?"

"No, but I know the hotel makes enough money to run itself and pay for the renovations."

"You don't know shit!" Andy angrily replied.

"I know enough to know that I will no longer deposit any more money in the business account." Tameka's response was firm. She did not bat an eye as she kept her eyes on the road.

Andy marinated on Tameka's response. He needed the money she deposited to help him sustain the comfortable life he made for himself in the Virgin Islands. He glanced at her and noticed the scowl on her face. "What's going on, Tameka?"

"Andy, we agreed to split the bills 50/50 when we first married." She glanced at him, before asking, "Do you remember?"

"Yeah, I remember. But with three kids to feed, how does your math add up?"

Tameka shook her head in disgust. "Don't give me that nonsense. I take care of the kids by myself. You haven't contributed anything to the household since you purchased that dilapidated hotel a year ago."

"But thanks to my hard work," Andy boasted with a silly grin on his face, "I have made it a five-star hotel, attracting celebrities around the world."

"Exactly!" Tameka snapped, gripping her hands on the steering wheel out of frustration. "The hotel makes enough money, but you're not contributing to your family."

"You never complained before. What is it with you and money?"

"I'm stressed out," Tameka conceded, after taking a deep breath and exhaling. "We have a new Director and it seems he's picked up where Cyrus Hampton left off."

Andy knew what Tameka was talking about. He was aware that his wife was a part of the scheme to defraud the federal government. "Are you under investigation?" he asked after a short pause.

"I don't know," she solemnly replied.

"What's the Director's name?"

Tameka glanced in her husband's direction while focusing on the traffic in front of her. "His name is Paul Alexander, but you don't know him."

"I'll take care of everything," Andy said, while thinking and cupping his chin.

"Andy, don't do anything stupid."

"Now I understand why you're angry. And don't worry, you're not going to jail."

Tameka felt comforted by her husband's concern. Her mood changed, and her anger toward him softened. "Sorry I mentioned the money, it's just...."

Andy showed her the palm of his hand to gesture a truce. "It's okay, babe. You know I wouldn't ask you the deposit the money if I didn't need it. I promise, in the very near future, you can stop making the deposits. In fact, you'll be able to retire, and I'll take care of you and the kids."

"Sounds great, Andy." *I heard that before*, she wanted to scream.

Tameka decided not to push the issue about her suspicion that her husband was conversing with a woman earlier. She feared he would get mad and leave without seeing the kids. She wanted to resume the conversation about their financial situation but Andy's eyes were closed.

Though, Andy was not taking a nap. He just wanted to give his wife the appearance that he was asleep. His mind was clouded with images of his mistress and their passionate love making encounters.

***

During the drive home, Tameka acknowledged the money she was receiving from fake pensioners was not enough to maintain their standard of living. The imbalance in their financial situation occurred after cyphering almost fifty percent of the embezzled money to help repair and renovate the hotel, which suffered structural damages during Hurricane Irma.

Although Tameka earned a six-figure salary at SCG, it was barely enough to pay the mortgage on a seven-hundred-thousand-dollar home, private school tuition for three kids, and payments for a luxury car. They were living above their means and something had to give. Tameka believed selling the hotel would be worth the sacrifice. All she had to do was convince her husband.

Chapter 27

Checkmate

The brief meeting with Tameka Collins-Brown had heavily weighed on Paul's mind. He needed to find a way to make her talk without feeling incriminated. He had intended on speaking with her again but was surprised to learn she was on scheduled leave.

In retrospect, the chain of events that occurred during the week dominated his attention. Some of the SCG staff members seemed to test his patience and made him wonder if they were intentionally trying to sabotage his efforts.

A former spy for the United States government had just retired and needed a new identity and pension. Paul was ill-prepared to debrief the agent because Eddie did not provide sufficient information to establish evidentiary documents. His deputy gave him the information only after Paul had asked for assistance from the White House.

Next, there was the issue with Stephanie McPherson, one of the Senior Writers responsible for creating new backgrounds for former spy agents. He had rejected her request to set up a new pensioner based on flimsy information. "You need more development on this case," he told her.

"What do you want from me?" Stephanie asked after sighing. "I've worked here a lot longer than you, and I know what I'm doing. I just need you to sign off on this request and let me do my job."

Paul leaned back in his office chair with his arms crossed. "You need to follow the chain of command."

"But Eddie told me that everything has to be approved by you."

Paul remembered giving his deputy that directive the prior week. "I'll tell you what – leave everything you have with me, and I'll let you know of my decision *ASAP*. Is that okay with you?"

Stephanie bit her bottom lip, trying to prevent from uttering another word.

"Are we in agreement?" Paul inquired for clarification.

Stephanie nodded before mumbling, "I guess so." She turned on her heels and left his office with fury.

After the Senior Writer left his office, Paul perused through the personnel files stacked on his desk to find Stephanie's. Her file was not in the stack. He thought it was odd, so he asked his Administrative Assistance to obtain the missing file.

Another matter involved Paul's inability to access the SCG system. He had made repeated complaints to the IT Team Leader that the system was riddled with bugs, which prevented him from accessing the database. Feigning ignorance, Barrett explained that he had the same access and did not have any problems accessing the system.

Paul checked his watch before responding. "I have a meeting in a few minutes. But when I return, I want you with me when I attempt to access the database. Just so you can have firsthand knowledge of the bugs. Do you get my drift?"

"I'm…. uh…I'm scheduled to leave early today," Barrett fumbled the words from his mouth.

Paul cocked his head sideways, letting Barrett know that he was not to be played with. Then he stood up and put on his suit jacket before turning his attention to his subordinate. "I'll see you first thing Monday. Otherwise, I'm putting you on notice that your job will be in jeopardy. Do you understand?"

Barrett nodded in a bouncy motion while averting his eyes to the floor.

"I'm glad we have an understanding," Paul commented, before pushing past Barrett to leave his office.

Dumbfounded and speechless, Barrett was scared for the first time since meeting his new Director. He thought about quitting his job but his gambling debt left him no other alternative. "Winning big is the key," he thought to himself. "I just need one good hand at Blackjack, and I'm out of here."

Chapter 28

Power Trip

The Chief Officer was true to his word. The next day he terminated Maria Hernandez' temporary promotion. He justified his actions by explaining to Human Resources that he wanted to install someone in her position with more experience and on a permanent basis. He also arranged for her to be transferred out of his department to a smaller branch in an offsite location. Then he requested that the guards at the Security station deactivate her access to the building.

Maria was oblivious to her Chief Officer's actions. She was feeling giddy as she drove to work. Brian had made her feel special after he had expressed his intentions to marry her. Besides sex, no one had ever shown any interest in getting to know her better.

After parking her car, she walked up the path to the front entrance. She tried using her access card to enter the building, but the door didn't click open. The guard opened the door for her and told her she had been transferred to an offsite location. He explained that he had to escort her to her office to retrieve her things.

Maria was about to protest before she recalled her Chief Officer's threat to take back her promotion. Her shoulders dropped and her eyes began to water.

Brian walked up from behind her, and asked, "What's going on?"

"That asshole!" she shouted.

"What are you talking about?"

"Our Chief Officer," she mumbled, before catching her breath. "He told me he was going to do this."

"Do what?"

"I don't know how to explain it." She was choked up, as tears fell from her eyes. "He took away my promotion and transferred me to the offsite location."

"Don't cry," Brian said as he retrieved a handkerchief from his suit pocket and handed it to her. He pondered Maria's dilemma before nodding in understanding. "Let's go with the guard to get your things out of the office. Then I'll go with you to your new office."

"You don't have to do this."

"But I do. Today is my last day at the Department of Defense, and I'd rather spend it helping my girlfriend."

Maria blushed while drying her tears with the handkerchief.

"So let me do this for you."

Brian made assumptions about what may have happened between Maria and the Chief Officer, but he needed to hear it from her. He wanted to be her knight in shining armor, even at the risk of subjecting himself to ridicule by onlookers and his superiors.

Dutifully, they followed the guards to Maria's office. Brian retrieved an empty box from the storage closet to help her box her things. He was impressed with the number of citations she received for her accomplishments. She had even received the Hammer Award, which was typically awarded to employees that implemented significant changes in the Department of Defense.

"Is that it?" he asked, after Maria placed a framed picture of her deceased mother in the box.

She nodded.

"Let's get out of here. This place doesn't deserve you."

Maria placed her hand on top of Brian's and looked into his eyes. "I have to tell you something."

"Does it have anything to do with the Chief Officer?"

She nodded in the affirmative.

"Well, I don't want to hear it. Whatever happened between you two is in the past, right?"

"It's just…I don't want you to judge me."

"I'm not in a position to judge you. I just want you to be okay. And I want you to be a part of my life. Do you feel the same?"

She smiled. "Yes."

"Am I the reason you are in this situation?"

At a loss for words, Maria bit her bottom lip and casted her eyes to the floor. In a soft tone, she explained, "I realize the promotion isn't worth it, if it meant that I have to sell my soul. I want to be with you. I…think I love you."

Brian instantly pulled her into his arms and kissed her passionately on the lips. Then he stood back and gazed into her eyes. "You just made me the happiest man in the world. I believe I have always loved you."

***

After Maria got settled in her new office, Brian returned to the Department of Defense to pack his things. He was ready to move on to the Select Committee for General Services. He submitted a leave slip to call it a day. Then he ran into the Chief Officer on his way out of the building.

The Chief Officer did not utter one word to Brian. Instead he stared him down as if he was a nothing, a nobody.

In response, Brian stood in one place and dared him to utter one word. His fists curled up as if he was ready for a fight. Then he bit his bottom lip and his brows crinkled as he bore a long unflinching gaze.

The Chief Officer took a step back in response. Then he averted his eyes and walked away.

Brian was furious when he exited the building and climbed behind the wheel of his Porsche. He wanted the Chief Officer to pay for how he treated Maria. But he also wanted his girlfriend to leave the past behind. Smiling inwardly, he believed her transfer was a mixed blessing and an opportunity for them to start anew.

Chapter 29

It Just Got Real

Paul finally had the opportunity to review Stephanie McPherson's personnel file. He was not impressed with his findings. It appeared to him that she lacked the qualifications to be a Senior Writer, a high-level position.

Within three years, Stephanie was promoted from a Secretary to Senior Writer, which was a seventy-thousand-dollar salary increase. Paul was perplexed when her file did not contain a college degree, like all the other personnel files he had reviewed so far. He frowned after noting Eddie had highly recommended Stephanie for the job.

Closing the file, Paul was mentally drained from trying to dissect or figure out how Stephanie obtained her position. He made a mental note to do some more research when he returned to work on Monday.

Thank God It's Friday! Paul wanted to shout as he shut down his computer. He put on his suit jacket, grabbed his briefcase, and departed his office. The icy stares from some SCG staff members no longer rattled him as he made his way to the elevator to go to the garage.

After climbing in his car, Paul decided to treat himself to an early dinner at the Rumor Mill restaurant in the Historic District of Ellicott City, one of the oldest cities in Howard County, Maryland. He parked his BMW at the metered parking space in front of the restaurant. Then he entered the restaurant and was pleasantly surprised he did not have to wait long to be serviced.

The waiter greeted Paul with a smile before escorting him to a table in the back. He was elated because it gave him the opportunity to enjoy his meal in quiet, away from the hustle and bustle of the Friday night crowd.

Passing on an appetizer, Paul ordered the rabbit ragu tossed with orecchiette pasta. For dessert, he devoured a French classic crème brulée, flavored with white chocolate & amaretto. A pot of fragrant green tea sealed the deal. It was all good as usual, so he left a generous tip.

Paul had no one and nothing to go home to, so he started a circuit on the main street, which consisted of art galleries, bakeries, boutiques, and bookstores. While scanning through the windows of the various shops, Paul fell behind a woman who was wearing black high heels, net stockings, a bright red scarf, and a too tight and too short blue dress. He was paying too close attention to her butt. She caught him by surprise when she abruptly turned around.

Startled, Paul noticed the woman's bright red lipstick matched her scarf. The woman's extra-large, dark sunglasses covered her eyes. She held a cigarette between her index and middle fingers before she held it to her mouth and took a long drag. Then she smiled and waved a cigarette toward him. Exhibiting a sexy Marilyn Monroe persona, she said in Spanish, "Hola Pablo, tiene un encendador?"

Paul froze in place trying to understand what the woman was asking. He knew a little Spanish from his college days, but the woman's question seemed bizarre. In his mind, she said, "Hello Paul, do you have a lighter?"

Who is this woman, and why is she calling me by my name? More importantly, why is she asking for a lighter when her cigarette is already lit?

Paul was getting ready to answer her question when suddenly, another woman snuck up from behind him and stuck him in the back with a long needle filled with chloroform. The woman was careful not to draw attention. Her physical features were semi-shielded by black slacks and shirt, dark sunglasses, and a scarf, which covered her head and was tied under her chin.

Immediately, Paul began to feel unsteady. Both women held him up before he went limp. Then they each took an elbow and guided him to a dark colored car. Soon it was lights out for *good ole* Paul.

"Mom, are you good?" Becky asked Stephanie, after she assisted with placing Paul in the front seat of her mother's car.

"Yes, I'm good," Stephanie confirmed after looking around to make sure no one was watching them. "Follow me in Paul's car. Here is his fob," she said, after she retrieved it from his pants pocket.

Three hours later, they crossed the City line into Waynesville, Pennsylvania, a little rural town outside of Harrisburg. Stephanie drove down a long, winding, unpaved road for thirty minutes before parking her car in a heavily wooded area. She waited for her daughter to park Paul's car behind hers. Then she climbed out of her car and surveyed the premises. She wanted to make sure no one was nearby.

Becky climbed out of Paul's car with reservations. She looked around the isolated area before she slowly approached her mother's car. "Mom," she said with fear in her voice, "we're not going to kill him, are we?"

"Don't be silly. I need you to help me get him out of my car." Stephanie shook her head. She could not understand how her daughter graduated in the top of her class but lacked good common sense. Unlike her younger daughter, who was autistic, Becky was dependable and always followed her commands.

"What are we going to do with him?" Becky inquired, fearing her mother would do the unthinkable.

"We're going to leave him right here."

"Are you serious?" Becky asked in amazement. "Out in the middle of *nowhere*?"

"Yep." Stephanie walked over to the passenger side of her car and opened the door. Then she grabbed Paul by the collar of his shirt and struggled to pull him out of the car. He was too heavy. She looked at her daughter who was still staring at her in disbelief. "Are you going to help or just stand there?"

Becky snapped out of her spell and ran over to help her mother drag Paul out of the car and onto the ground. She stood back and watched her mother work quickly to remove Paul's clothes.

Unlike her daughter, Stephanie's confidence was at an all-time high. She had a feeling this scare tactic would work. Smiling on the inside, she thought, *SCG is going to have one less Director on Monday, and everything will return to normal.*

Chapter 30

Unhinged

Tameka and her family were eating dinner when her husband's cell phone began to ring. She became suspicious when Andy retrieved his cell phone from his pocket to answer it. Then she became angry when he left the table and went into the living room to talk. Shortly afterward, the kids asked to be excused after they finished eating dinner. They went out in the backyard to play. But Tameka remained seated at the table, waiting for her husband to return.

"Who was that on the phone?" she asked, after Andy entered the dining room with a big smile on his face.

"The hotel. I have to fly back this evening." Andy sat at the table to resume eating.

"Why?"

Between bites, Andy explained, "There is an emergency at the hotel. Gotta be there to handle some issues." He was partially telling the truth. The former beauty pageant had called and told him his absence from her bed was deemed an emergency.

Tameka wanted to inquire further but piecing together her husband's short answers was equivalent to pulling teeth. She noticed her husband finished eating his plate of food and drank his glass of iced tea. He did not utter a word when he stood up and went upstairs to their bedroom.

Feeling deflated, Tameka cleared the table, washed the dishes and went upstairs to join her husband. She sat on their bed to watch him pack his clothes for the trip back to the Virgin Islands. "Andy, I need to talk to you."

"About what?"

"My co-worker, Stephanie McPherson wants me to create fake pensioners for her even though our deputy told us not to."

"Are you serious?" Andy quizzed while continuing to pack his things. "I wouldn't do it if I were you. If anything, you should create some more accounts for us. We can use the money."

Shaking her head, Tameka stood up and pouted. "Did you not understand that my new Director is investigating fraud at my job."

"I told you not to worry about him. I'll make sure he's not a problem.

"And how are you going to do that from the Virgin Islands?"

"Just leave everything to me," Andy explained as he finished packing his suitcase.

Tameka was worried. She did not want to be alone, especially after her last meeting with Paul. "Honey, I don't understand why you are leaving so soon. You've only been home a couple of days."

"I told you there is an emergency I have to deal with at the hotel."

"When are you coming back home?"

"Soon."

"But when?"

"Don't aggravate me, woman!" Andy's harsh tone was followed by a cold stare meant to scare Tameka into submission.

Fearing backlash, Tameka did not press the issue. She bit her bottom lip and glanced down at the floor.

Suddenly, there was a knock at the front door. They looked at each other in bewilderment, before Andy asked, "Are you expecting someone?"

"No."

"Check who's at the door while I finish packing."

Tameka rolled her eyes at her husband before she strolled downstairs to open the door. It was the FBI.

"Are you Tameka Collins-Brown?" the agent asked.

"Yes, I'm Tameka. May I help you?"

"I'd like to ask you some questions about Cyrus Hampton. Can we come inside?"

"Uh…sure," Tameka said, as she stood back to let the agents enter her home. "You can have a seat." She pointed to the plush white sofa in the guest room. Then she sat in the side chair facing the sofa.

One agent stood near the front door and the other agent sat on the sofa and retrieved a small tablet and pen from his front shirt pocket. Prepared to take notes, he began by stating, "We need to know your whereabouts the night Cyrus Hampton was murdered.

"I was out with my colleague at a play in DC."

"Do you remember what time the play started and ended?" Tameka was about to respond when her husband strutted downstairs with his suitcase.

Andy glanced at the agents, before asking Tameka, "Are you still taking me to the airport?"

"Um…" Tameka turned to the agents before responding to her husband. "The FBI is investigating my former Director's murder. They are here to ask me questions."

"I gotta go to the airport. Can y'all come back later?"

The agents stared at Andy in disbelief. "We only have a few questions. Do you mind?"

"Yes, I do. I have a plane to catch. Are y'all going to fly me to my destination if I miss my plane?" Andy's demeanor was indignant and embarrassing for Tameka.

"I apologize, sir," one of the FBI agents replied. "I did not know this was an inopportune time. We can come back later." He retrieved a business card from his wallet and handed it to Tameka. "Or you can give me a call when you get a chance."

"Okay."

"She'll call you later," Andy butted in. "Come on, Tameka. I gotta go."

Tameka turned to the agent and mouthed, "I'm so sorry."

The agent nodded. "It's okay. I look forward to your call."

As soon as the agents left, Tameka turned to her husband to chastise him for his behavior. The frown on his face told her it would not be prudent. Instead, she said, "I'll take you to the airport." She grabbed her car keys and purse and headed out the front door.

Andy smirked. "That's what I'm talking about."

Tameka took Andy to the airport without muttering a single word.

Andy did not seem to mind the quiet noise, as he was on his cell phone texting the whole time. He did not even bother giving Tameka a kiss before climbing out of the car.

When Tameka hit the button to open the trunk, Andy retrieved his suitcase and walked inside the airport without looking back. She shook her head after recalling his subliminal threats against the SCG Director. *How are you going to take care of Paul when you are headed to one of the most beautiful places on Earth?*

Chapter 31

Collaboration

Stephanie dusted off her knees after she and her daughter dragged an unconscious Paul Alexander to an area void of homes. However, the area was populated with wild animals and overgrown trees. Stephanie was satisfied her Director would not be alive before the weekend was over. She glanced at her daughter who was eerily quiet. "Are you okay?" she asked with genuine concern.

Becky nodded in the affirmative but she lied. "Mom, what's going to happen to him?"

Stephanie shrugged. "I don't know." Though, she was certain Paul would be eaten by bears or accidentally shot by wildlife hunters.

"What are we going to do now?" Becky asked.

"We have to get rid of his car. I have a plan. Follow me in his car." Stephanie climbed in her car and started the ignition. She waited for her daughter to start Paul's car, before driving southbound. It took a half an hour before they drove onto the main highway.

Two hours later, they parked the cars in front of their farm in Adamstown, Maryland. Stephanie climbed out of her car but could not understand why Becky did not follow her lead. She approached Paul's car, before asking, "Are you coming inside?"

Becky looked up at her mom and shook her head. "I'm confused. Why did we drive his car here?"

"We are out in the middle of nowhere. No one will be able to locate Paul's car out here."

"What if he has a tracking device on his car?"

"Damn!" Stephanie grimaced. She did not think that far ahead. "Becky, you went to school for engineering. Can you remove the tracking device?"

"Yeah, I think I can. I need a few minutes to create a GPS blocker but it only works over a short range and when it's plugged into the power supply in the car."

"Will it erase the prior locations?"

"Yes."

"Well, don't just sit in the car! We need to hurry up and get a move on!"

Becky dutifully obliged her mother's request. It took less than fifteen minutes for her to create a GPS blocker. She sighed with relief.

"It's works," Stephanie said after taking a deep breath and exhaling. "Now we have to take his car to Brookeville, Maryland."

Becky frowned after realizing Paul resided in Brookeville. "Are you sure you want to take his car to his home?"

"No, but the Patuxent River State Park is near his home. If we hide his car there, it will take months before anyone find it."

Becky was tired and hungry. She was also doubtful of her mother's plans. But she knew not to argue when her mom was riled up.

Almost two hours later, they arrived at their intended destination. Stephanie did not use the park entrances. Instead, she drove in the surrounding areas of the park, and located a small opening near the river. The area was mountainous and surrounded by lush greenery. Besides the steady flow of water from the stream, it was eerily quiet and serene.

Stephanie climbed out of the car and canvassed the area. She wanted to make sure no one was around. Then she walked over by the water to gauge whether it was deep enough to hide a car.

Becky climbed out of Paul's car and walked over to her mother. "What are we going to do?"

"We are going to drive the car in the river."

Becky shook her head. "This is not going to work. I don't think the water is deep enough. A kayaker or hiker is sure to find it."

Exasperated, Stephanie turned to her daughter with fiery eyes. "What do you suggest?"

"The bushes and trees are high enough in this area to conceal the car." Becky looked over at the trees that were leaning over. "We can hide the car over there."

"That's a great idea."

For the next few minutes, the ladies worked together to hide Paul's car in the trees and bushes. Then they made sure to wipe away their fingerprints from the steering wheel and door handle.

Stephanie was satisfied the car would not be discovered before fall, when all the leaves start shedding.

"Mom, the GPS blocker won't work if the car is turned off."

"That's fine, as long as the GSP tracker won't be able to detect our prior locations."

"No it won't," Becky replied with confidence. "Now what?"

"We have to make a quick detour to Paul's home to drop off his belongings. Then we go home and pretend this never happened."

Becky bit her bottom lip to refrain from protesting the next plan of action. She had a feeling her mother's bad decisions would come back to haunt both of them some day.

In contrast, Stephanie was feeling invigorated. She paid attention to the scenery as she and Becky were leaving Patuxent River. She recollected the time when she and her family spent many summers hiking at the State Park. *It is still beautiful*, she thought to herself.

Chapter 32

Fractured Vows

After Tameka dropped Andy off at the airport, she opted to do some research on her husband. Her gut instincts told her he was cheating on her. She needed to know who her husband was talking to from the moment he arrived home until the moment he left to return to the Virgin Islands. She was able to access his cell phone records because their cell phones were under the same AT&T family plan.

She noticed a phone number Andy frequently called in the past few days. Then she located past phone bills and noticed the same phone number appearing numerous times for the past six months. She was curious, so she picked up her cell phone to call the mystery person.

A woman answered the phone on the second ring. Tameka titled her head sideways, before asking, "Uh.... who is this?"

"Who is this?" the woman countered.

"Mrs. Tameka Collins-Brown."

"I see," the woman stated after realizing Andy's wife was the caller. "Though, I'm not sure why you are calling me, or how you got my number."

"I'm calling to inquire about my husband."

"I can't help you."

"Are you sleeping with my husband?" Tameka was met with silence, so she asked, "Did you hear me?"

"You need to talk to him."

Then there was a long pause before Andy got on the phone. "Tameka, why are you calling random strangers?"

"I'm not an idiot!" Tameka snapped. "Are you sleeping with her?"

"Let's talk about this when I return home."

"I will no longer live a lie. If you can't tell me you're not sleeping with her, there is nothing to talk about!" She hit the END Call button on her cell when Andy did not refute her suspicions.

Tameka was overcome with rage. She screamed so loud, it startled her son, who was in his bedroom next to hers. He ran into her room and found her on the floor next to her bed crying profusely.

"Mommy, what's wrong?" her seven-year-old son asked as he sat next to her with his head on her chest.

"I'm fine," she said between sniffles. "I'm so sorry I woke you. Let's get you back in bed."

Tameka stood up and held her son's hand when she escorted him to his room. "Don't worry, I'm going to be fine." Then she tucked him in bed and kissed him on the forehead. "Good night, sweetheart."

She returned to her bedroom and closed the door behind her. Then she laid across her king-size bed and cried in peace. Her chest was aching from a broken heart.

Chapter 33

Nervous Energy

Eddie's wife noticed he had been unusually quiet. For the past two weeks, he would come home, chuck back beer like water, and stretch out on the recliner. He would turn on the TV but never watch an entire program. Then he would take a shower, go to bed, wake up the next morning, and start the routine all over again.

MaryJo thought it was unusual for her husband not to blast the TV with his favorite sports channels. She sat on the sofa next to his recliner and stared into his face. There were heavy bags under his eyes.

Sensing human presence, Eddie opened his eyes and quickly sat up in the recliner. "Honey, are you okay?"

"Eddie, you haven't been yourself lately. Is everything okay at work?"

"I'm okay, MaryJo. Don't worry."

"Don't shut me out. Please tell me what's going on."

Eddie shook his head, took a deep breath, and blew out air in frustration. "It's Stephanie McPherson."

"What did she do this time?" Eddie had already told MaryJo that Stephanie was disappointed when she could not get approval to open an account for a new fake pensioner.

"I think she's paranoid. She's going to mess around and get all of us in trouble."

"Do you think Stephanie had anything to do with Cyrus Hampton's death?"

Eddie frowned. "I don't think so. Stephanie told me she was at a play in DC with Tameka when he was murdered."

"Has anyone from the FBI contacted you yet?"

Eddie hesitated before responding. "Yes, they did. But don't worry. They are interviewing everyone at SCG."

"What did they say?"

"They wanted to know of my whereabouts the night the Director was murdered."

"What did you tell them?"

Eddie looked at his wife with furrowed brows. "What do you mean? I was here with you."

"Okay." MaryJo distinctly remembered her husband told her he was going to be late getting home that night, because he was going to a bar with a colleague to celebrate his birthday.

"Um...you were here with me that night," she lied to appease her husband. "What about Stephanie? What did she do?"

"I'll take care of Stephanie. Try not to worry."

Shaking her head in despair, MaryJo was more than worried. She was fully aware of the scheme at SCG, and she was fully aware of her husband's involvement.

Six months earlier, Eddie had invested in a pyramid scheme. MaryJo had warned him that the investment

144

opportunity sounded too good to be true, but he wouldn't listen to her. Eddie wanted to believe that he could double their savings, including the money they received from the fake pensioners. He ended up being sucked into investing more money, only to discover he was being bamboozled. He worked tirelessly to return the money to all the investors that he had encouraged to join him in the pyramid scheme.

"What about Michael's tuition?" MaryJo inquired.

"I got that covered." Eddie shivered at the thought of not being able to afford to put their only child through college. "I've made arrangements with the school to send monthly payments."

"Michael will receive his bachelor's degree in six months. How are we going to pay for his graduate program?"

"I'll find a way."

MaryJo never thought her husband would resort to embezzling money from the government. At the time, she reasoned he had good cause. Now she was having second thoughts. She looked at her husband with sad eyes. Nervous energy permeated their home.

Blowing out air in frustration, Eddie was also bent out of shape after discussing the ordeal with his wife. It did not help that his wife was worried sick about his involvement in the SCG investigation. He knew he had to do something to put her mind at ease.

"I'll be back," he told his wife as he grabbed his car keys and wallet."

"Where are you going?"

"I'm going to make sure our future remains intact." He approached her and kissed her on the forehead, before telling her, "We're going to be fine. No one is going to jail, because the Director is never going to find what he's looking for."

MaryJo watched her husband disappear into the garage. Her focus shifted to the floor when she heard his car's ignition. "God help us," she whispered aloud.

Chapter 34

Left for Dead

Paul woke up to the sounds of insects and birds. He was on the ground in a desolate area. Flies were working on an animal nearby and yet another was smelly and had been eaten by vultures. Dressed in underclothes only, he was laying on his back and wrapped in a blue synthetic tarp.

Neatly arranged nearby were his wallet, watch, and loose change. He looked in his wallet and was relieved to see his driver's license, credit cards and cash. There was also a stack of clothes: camo pants and matching shirt, a gimme hat, a canteen, and boots-no socks.

Paul was thirsty so he started to unscrew the canteen to see what liquid it held. He hesitated when thoughts of poisoned smoothies danced through his muddled brain. *But that's how Cyrus Hampton was murdered!* Suddenly, staying thirsty was not a bad idea. He put the screw back on the canteen and placed it on the ground.

The flies continued to buzz, but the birds flapped away. He noticed the trees looked a little ragged. "But…so what!" Paul exclaimed. *What I want to know is why am I undressed in the woods and left with some of my stuff and some of someone else's stuff?*

He stood up, ridded his body of the blue tarp and slipped on the pants and shirt. He looked around but did not see any socks. There was a pocketknife and two energy bars on the ground nearby. After deciding not to eat the food, he sat on the blue tarp to put on the boots which were too large. Shaking his head, he thought to himself, *Large boots without socks equal blisters on my feet.*

"Great," he said aloud. "I don't know where I am. I am thirsty. My head hurts. I'm surrounded by dead animals and overgrown trees that look like a war zone. Why?"

Paul started to stand up, but he dropped down when a volley of gun shots ripped through the trees. From the sound, multiple people were firing heavy duty automatic weapons. He sighed with relief, after solving the mystery of the ragged trees and the dead animals.

He fumbled around looking for his cell phone but could not find it. He noticed his car fob and house keys were missing from his key ring. Even if the car was nearby, he could not start it unless the devils, who left him for dead, left the car fob in the car.

Thinking long and hard about his kidnappers, he distinctly remembered the woman with bright red lipstick. Her eyes were shielded with dark sunglasses and she was wearing a sexy outfit, which was unusual attire when frequenting the historic market district in Ellicott City, Maryland.

Paul considered crawling to a lower spot when the shooting stopped. He soon discovered the mystery of the blue tarp. The low spots in the tarp were wet, but he was too scared to be ashamed of peeing on himself.

The shooting started again. It would not be good to stand up and run, and crawling would be nasty. If he had reliable food and water, he would just stay low and wait. But, if he waited too long, the summer sun would make him into a crispy critter.

The shooting stopped again. Paul decided that when he did move, it would be only a few steps at a time. There was no set interval between volleys. Next decision – left or right. Safe ground should not be far, Paul surmised, after considering his weight and all the stuff the kidnappers had left for his use.

Which direction should I go, left or right? Mentally, Paul flipped a coin in his head, and the left won. He gathered his meager possessions, including the suspect water and energy bars, and took five steps during each quiet period.

Turning left was a good choice because he came upon a road guarded by a water-filled ditch and a barbed-wire fence. His feet hurt, but he was dry. He was also scratched up but not cut. He went in the direction of the shooting, looking for a narrow place that would lead him to the road.

Paul soon walked into a private gun club full of heavy weapons and gun *nuts*. They were nice gun nuts, Paul determined, after greeting them with a nod and nervous smile. They gave him food and cold water. He gleaned from their brief encounter that he was in Reading, Pennsylvania.

One of the guys allowed him to fire a full magazine of a highly customized AR-15. Paul could not believe that there was still ammo available for the 1921 U. S. Navy Thompson model. To fit in with the locals, he fired some of the ammo down range but at nothing in particular.

Then one of the guys, who was meeting family in Hershey, Pennsylvania, offered to take him to the Philadelphia airport. On the hour and half drive to Philadelphia, Paul and his new friend talked about guns, the weather, and the stock market. His new friend did not ask him how he got there, nor did Paul volunteer any information about the strange circumstances of his abduction.

When they were not talking, Paul thought about his assailants. He believed they were very thoughtful but mean-spirited. In a fleeting moment, he thought about how he would torture them to death if he ever discovered who they were. The likelihood of that happening was slim to none, but at least it kept Paul occupied for a while.

Chapter 35

Ties that Bind

After assuring his wife that his Director's SCG investigation would not uncover the fraud scheme, Eddie Rosenthal sent a group text message to specific SCG staff before he drove to the Veterans of Foreign Wars club in Alexandria, Virginia. He sat at the bar and drank a beer. Then he headed to the conference room in the back of the club.

While sitting at the head of the conference table, Eddie thought about the investigation. He realized he couldn't guarantee that everyone involved would not be in criminal jeopardy. He thought someone had to be the sacrificial lamb, but he was doubtful he would be able to get any takers.

Thirty minutes later, SCG's Administrative Assistant, Sally Bates showed up at the VFW. She entered the conference room and noticed the Deputy Director was sweating profusely and his clothes looked disheveled.

"What in the hell is a matter with you?" she asked Eddie as she sat in the chair next to him.

Eddie wiped the sweat from his forehead, before explaining, "I'm having a bad day."

"What's up with the text message? Do you know what time it is?"

He gazed at Sally, before replying, "I would not have sent it if it was not important."

She grimaced before canvassing the empty room. Then she turned to Eddie, and asked, "When are the others going to get here?"

"Everyone confirmed that they will be here soon." He checked his watch and sighed.

Sally looked at him and shook her head in disgust. "Eddie, you need to get it together before everyone else gets here. We need to show confidence, but you are showing weakness."

"Look Sally, it's because of me, none of us landed in jail when Cyrus Hampton was alive. So give me a break."

"Get it together," Sally snapped followed by a sharp gaze.

Eddie rolled his eyes just as the IT Team Leader walked into the conference room.

"What is this about?" Barrett Pike asked as he sat in the chair opposite of Sally's.

"I'll tell you when everyone else gets here."

"Fine with me. I'm going to get a beer. You want one?" he asked Eddie.

"No he doesn't," Sally interjected. "We need Eddie to be sober when everyone else arrives."

Thirty minutes later, Tameka entered the conference room with red teary eyes. Her shoulders were slumped over and she walked as if the whole world was crashing down around her. "I had to call a babysitter to...." Her voice trailed off because she was trying to stifle her tears.

Sally stood up and approached Tameka. Then she held her hand, before asking, "Are you okay?"

"I'm fine. But my marriage…." Tameka burst out in tears before she was able to admit that her marriage was on the rocks. "And the FBI…." Again, her sentence was incomplete. She wanted to tell them the FBI had contacted her about Cyrus Hampton's murder, but tears started flowing from her eyes.

"Now, now, dear," Sally said in a soothing voice. "We all have problems, but you have to be strong. Whatever it is, it can always be worse. You are talking to someone that lost a child and two husbands to cancer. So trust me when I tell you that you will be fine. Have faith and know that you will survive your current circumstances."

Tameka nodded in agreement as she dried her tears with the handkerchief she had used before arriving at the VFW. "I'm sorry I'm not as strong as you."

"But you are. Keep your head up."

Tameka turned to Eddie to apologize for being late to the meeting.

"You're not the only one," Barrett grumbled while entering the room and checking his watch.

"Where is she?" Eddie said aloud.

"I'm sure Stephanie will be here soon," Sally replied, before she turned to Tameka. "Have a seat, dear."

Tameka nodded before she sat in the chair next to Sally.

"I'm going to call her," Eddie said aloud before he retrieved his cell phone out of his pocket. "Where are you?" he angrily asked when Stephanie answered his call.

"I'm on my way. I was stuck in traffic," she lied, to ease the tension. Truth was – Stephanie was at the gas station filling her tank after traveling from Maryland to Pennsylvania earlier. "I should be there in fifteen minutes."

Stephanie disconnected the call before Eddie started whining about her tardiness. Being late was the least of her worries. She was sleep deprived and her belly was empty. Her energy was at an all-time low, but her adrenaline never withered. Stephanie was fighting for her children, her finances, and her livelihood. She was ready to kill – as a last resort, if necessary.

Chapter 36

Homebound

Paul's arrival at the Philadelphia airport was the beginning to the end of a nightmare. He thanked the gun nut for the ride, and they exchanged phone numbers to stay in touch. Though, Paul had a feeling that would be his last time seeing the man that made his life rebound.

Upon entering the airport, he bought a plane ticket to go to the BWI airport in Maryland. Then he visited a retail store and bought a short-sleeve polo shirt, a pair of Dickie slacks, a comb, toothbrush and toothpaste, deodorant, and body wipes. After paying for the items, he went into the restroom to wash up and put on his new clothes. He wanted to look as inconspicuous as possible.

He thought about buying a cell phone but remembered he kept a second cell phone at home with all his contacts. Besides, he thought it would be best if no one knew about his torment until he returned home.

Feeling and looking refreshed, Paul found an ATM and withdrew five hundred dollars. He believed the cost of revenge was going up in monetary terms. Though, the one-hour flight home made up for the financial loss.

Because he did not have any bags, he was able to walk out the airport and wait for a taxi. A taxi drove up within seconds. He gave the driver his home address, then rested his head on the headrest. Exhausted, Paul closed his eyes and took a light nap.

The taxi driver arrived at his home forty minutes later. "Sir," he said to his sleeping passenger, "we're here."

Paul stifled his yawned before climbing out the backseat of the cab. He walked around to the driver's side and paid the driver one-hundred dollars. "Keep the change."

"Thank you." The driver's smile showed he was grateful for the generous tip.

Paul waited for the taxi to leave before he walked around the back of his home to get the spare key, which he hid under the planter on the back porch. He looked around to make sure no one was watching before he bent down to retrieve it.

After opening the back door, Paul's heart was beating at a rapid pace as he inspected his home to make sure no one was lurking inside. His heartbeat returned to normal after noticing everything was intact. Just inside the front door were the socks he wore when he was kidnapped.

He looked closely and noticed the socks contained items that made them appear lumpy. In slow motion, he dug inside the socks to retrieve the contents. One had his car fob and house key, and the other had his cell phone.

The front door was unlocked, so he rushed to lock it. Then he pried the cell phone open and was relieved the sim card was still there. Though, the battery was completed dead.

While the phone was charging, Paul went into the kitchen to fix a ham sandwich. He realized he could not think clearly on an empty stomach. The cell phone was fully charged by the time he washed his sandwich down with a cold bottle of water.

"Now what?" Paul thought aloud after pressing the button to turn the phone on. "I have to find my car." He scrolled through the contacts on his cell phone and contacted the Smart Alert service. This was his first time ever using the GPS tracking service. It was also the first time his car was stolen since he purchased it as a retirement gift three years earlier.

The Smart Alert system instructed Paul on how to retrieve the location of his car on his cell phone. His eyes grew wide after discovering his car was less than fifteen minutes from his home. *How is that even possible? What is going on? Did they want me to find my car? Is this a setup? Maybe I should call the police.*

Paul stood up and paced his living room floor. He had to be sure he was not being deceived.

After changing into his hiking attire, he put on his Timberlands, grabbed his cell phone and car fob, and headed out the front door. Hiking was second nature to Paul, so he believed the fifteen-minute hike would be a breeze.

He arrived at the vicinity of where his car was traced and was disappointed when he did not find his car. *Where in the hell is it?* He walked over near the water and saw a whole bunch of tree limbs and bushes in a hilly pile. Looking closer, Paul noticed a Maryland tag plate peering from the bottom of the rubble.

"Is that what I think it is?" Paul pondered as he moved toward the license plate. He removed all the tree limbs and branches and was surprised to discover his car.

With the fob in his hand, Paul pressed the ignition and the car instantly started. He was happy, relieved, and bewildered all at the same time. He looked around to see if anyone else was in the vicinity – just in case he was being pranked.

Then he climbed behind the wheel of his car and slowly eased the car away from the rubble. He stopped the car and held his breath for second, after thinking that someone may have planted a bomb in his car. Then he chuckled. *I would have blown up a long time ago – if that were the case. The brakes and the steering wheel seem to be okay.*

Paul avoided returning home with his car. He did not want his kidnappers to know that he had survived their torment. Retrieving his cell phone from his pocket, he called his friend, Brian Jeffs, to let him know he was on his way. Then he called Liz and gave her a brief version of his ordeal.

"Are you okay?" Liz asked.

"Yeah," Paul admitted with disbelief. "I'm not sure what my kidnappers were trying to achieve. Did they leave me for dead, or did they want to just torment me?"

"I'm confused as well. I think we should let the FBI know what's going on. Clearly, your life is in danger."

"Not yet. We agreed to keep the SCG investigation low key. So I'm the sacrificial lamb," he added with a chuckle. "Besides, I think I'm making headway in the SCG investigation."

"You have one week. Then I'm calling in the FBI and the CIA."

"I'll let you know if things get too hairy. I gotta go," Paul added, after he spotted Brian in front of his home.

Chapter 37

Confessionals

Stephanie arrived at the VFW just as the IT Team Leader threatened to leave. She looked tired and haggard. Everyone noticed she was unusually quiet. Typically, she would enter the room, greeting everyone with fake smiles and niceties. She sat in the chair next to Barrett and looked at the empty chair across from her.

"Are you okay?" Barrett asked.

Stephanie took a deep breath and exhaled. "I feel like I've been in a war and barely survived."

"What did you do?" Tameka asked in an accusatory tone.

"Stephanie," Eddie interjected with furrowed brows, "did you do anything to Paul Alexander?"

She opened her mouth to speak but quickly closed it after everyone shot daggers in her direction.

Barrett banged his fist on the table, before screaming at everyone in the room, "This bitch is going to get us all locked up!" Then he addressed Stephanie with slanted eyes. "We all know it was you that flattened the Director's tire. What did you do now?"

Stephanie gathered her strength and leaned toward Barrett, barely touching his nose. Through gritted teeth, she said, "I was woman enough to do what you can never do, so don't fuck with me. Not today!"

"Now, now," Sally said to both Stephanie and Barrett, "there is no need to go to war with one another. A house divided will fall, but together, we can accomplish anything."

"I agree," Eddie admitted. "Now is the time to stick together. We should all go around the table to tell what we know about the SCG probe, and state what we did to thwart the investigation." He turned to Stephanie before adding, "We should also admit what we did to ensure we do not go to jail for incompetence."

"What do you mean by that?" Stephanie sneered at Eddie.

Sally held up her hands to silence Eddie. "He means nothing. I'll go first."

Eddie nodded. "Okay."

Sally cleared her throat before she began. "I discovered that the Director is serious about the SCG investigation. Paul requested that I obtain some personnel files, in addition to the files Eddie had given him. On more than one occasion, I saw him reviewing Tameka and Eddie's files."

Barrett frowned. "Why was he doing that?"

Sally said, "It makes sense. Tameka and Eddie have been signing off on all the pensioners since Cyrus terminated everyone else's access."

"Is there anything else we should know?" Barrett egged on.

"Paul recently asked me to get a copy of Stephanie's file." Then she turned to Eddie, and said, "I assume her file was not included in the batches you gave him."

Eddie nodded after acknowledging her assumption was correct. "Is there anything else?"

Sally shook her head. "Not really. For the most part, Paul has been secretive. He keeps his office door closed most of the day. But I don't believe he knows about the fake pensioners."

"Well, that bit of information is useful," Eddie said before he turned to Barrett. "Can you give us any information?"

"Sure," Barrett said as he sat on the edge of his chair. "Paul requested data on all pensioners for the past five years, but I purposely excluded the fake pensioners that are active."

"That's good." Eddie breathed a sigh of relief. "Anything else you have to share?"

Barrett nodded. "Paul specifically asked for the list of pensioners that Eddie and Tameka approved."

"That makes sense," Sally said. "Because, as I stated before, they are the only two SCG staff members that can approve the pensioners."

"Is that all?" Eddie asked Barrett.

"Paul asked for direct access to the database, but I've been stalling him."

"Is there any way to remove the fake pensioners?"

"Sure, but the benefits will also cease."

"That can't happen!" Stephanie shouted out.

Eddie frowned at Stephanie's reaction. "Please settle down. Terminating the benefits is the only way to make sure Paul doesn't discover our criminal activity."

"I don't know about that," Sally said. "Any interruption in benefits would draw attention to the discrepancy, especially if Paul performs a trend analysis on the total number of beneficiaries versus benefits paid."

"What should I do?" Barrett asked.

"Keep stalling him," Eddie replied, before turning to everyone else. "This is a tough one, guys. Put your thinking caps on until Barrett can figure out how to manipulate the data without drawing attention to the discrepancy." Then he looked around the room, and asked, "Is there anyone else that want to share information that can be useful?"

"I'll go next," Tameka volunteered. She paused, before admitting, "I believe Paul knows about the criminal activity at SCG."

"How do you know?" Eddie and Stephanie asked at the same time.

"I don't know for sure, but he told me to come clean with everything I know."

Sally shook her head and snickered. "That doesn't mean he knows anything."

Tameka turned to Stephanie, and said, "He will if you insist that I create two more fake pensioners for you."

"What are you talking about!" Eddie shouted, spit spraying out of his mouth from anger. "I thought I told both of you not to create any more accounts."

"I need the money," Stephanie pleaded. "You don't understand what is necessary to raise horses."

"Are you serious?" Barrett looked at Stephanie with disdain. "You want Tameka to create accounts for your damn horses. If you can't afford them, sell them! I'm not going to jail over no damn horses!"

"You don't understand," Stephanie started.

"No," Eddie responded with clinched teeth and narrowed eyes. "Whatever you have to say, I don't want to hear it. No more accounts!"

Stephanie held back tears that were welling up in her eyes. Her voice cracked, as she explained, "If this...is about Paul Alexander, you don't have to worry."

"What...did...you...do?" Eddie's words were choppy and laced with fear.

"I got rid of him."

"Aww...damn!" Barrett exclaimed as he slammed his hand on the conference table.

"I can't believe this!" Tameka cried out. "We are going to jail."

"No, we're not," Sally said with authority. "Everyone needs to calm down."

"Did you kill him?" Eddie asked Stephanie.

"Not exactly."

"From the beginning," Eddie said in a tone that meant to scare the living crap out of Stephanie. "Tell me everything you've done to Paul Alexander."

Over the next twenty minutes, Stephanie admitted that she flattened Paul's tire. She also explained how she recruited her eldest daughter to help her scare Paul with fake snake transmitters. And when that did not work, she explained how she and her daughter kidnapped Paul and left him for dead in the middle of nowhere.

Everyone sat there stunned after Stephanie finished her spiel. The likelihood of going to jail was on everyone's minds.

Also, in that very moment, almost everyone in the room believed Stephanie murdered Cyrus Hampton.

Eddie sighed. "People, we have to hang tough. Cyrus did not suspect pensioners because he approved nearly all of them. I generally only approved the pensioners when he was absent and Sally covered for me."

Tameka nodded before adding her two cents. "Stephanie and I are vulnerable on the pensioner issue because she writes the scenarios for the evidentiary documents, and I pre-approve them."

"Don't worry," Barrett said in response. "I have your back. Let's think about how to help Stephanie so she doesn't cause the shit to get stinkier." Then he looked at Stephanie through slanted eyes. "We should be okay unless one of us kills Cyrus Hampton."

Chapter 38

Batman and Robin

When Brian invited Paul into his home, he noticed his friend seemed timid and scared. He never witnessed his buddy in this condition. "You want something to drink?" he asked, after Paul sat on the bar stool in the kitchen.

"No, I'm good."

"Are you sure? You look kinda spooked."

"I have never been in this situation. This is the craziest thing that ever happened to me."

"Tell me what happened."

"You won't believe it."

"Tell me anyway."

Brian listened attentively as Paul recalled every detail of his kidnapping, including finding his car fifteen minutes from his home.

Paul also explained his uneasiness about going home. Shaking his head, he said, "Can you believe my kidnappers had the nerve to leave a granola bar?"

Stumped for words, Brian tried to talk but he was in shock from the story he had just heard. "You are right," he finally said. "That is one of the craziest stories I have ever heard in my entire life."

"I just don't know what to do at this point."

"Do you know who would want to harm you?"

"I don't have any enemies that I know of. The only thing I can think of is that my abduction may be related to the SCG investigation."

Brian frowned. "What are you talking about?"

Paul paused for minute before admitting why he was sent to SCG. He also told Brian about the evidentiary items he found in Cyrus Hampton's safe. "I think I have a lead, but she has not broken yet."

"She works for SCG?"

"Yes, and that's all I can tell you for now."

"Do you think anyone else is involved?"

"I'm not sure."

"What if you don't go to work on Monday?"

"How is my absence going to help me figure out who kidnapped me?"

"I'm supposed to report to SCG on Monday. Let me ask around and get a feel for what the SCG staff members might reveal."

"That's a good idea. I'll go to the White House on Monday, to meet with Jimmy to discuss the evidentiary items I found in the safe. I'll also inquire about the transmitters we discovered outside my house."

Brian frowned. "White House? Jimmy?"

Paul allowed Brian's one-word questions to linger. He knew he had to come clean. "The President and I are good friends. She recruited me to investigate whether fraudulent activity was taking place at SCG after the Director was murdered. Jimmy Johnson is her advisor."

Brian's mouth opened and eyes grew big. He timidly asked, "You personally know the President of the United States of America?"

"Yeah, she and I met in law school, and we've been friends ever since." Paul refrained from telling his younger friend that he and the President were actually friends with benefits back in the hay days.

"But you never told me."

"I never told anyone.

"So...is this how I got my job at SCG?"

Paul smirked. "Are you disappointed?"

"Hell no." Brian sat on the stool next to Paul and playfully punched him on the shoulder. "Your secret's safe with me. We're buddies for life."

"Yeah, like Batman and Robin."

In response, they boiled over from laughter.

Chapter 39

Voice of Reason

The Administrative Assistant, Sally left the VFW shortly after Tameka went home. She told the rest of the pact that she had to go home to feed her dogs. Truth was – she could no longer stand to be in their presence. She believed they were imbeciles. Sally was doubtful as everyone made a commitment to stick together and not snitch on each other regardless of the outcome.

Cringing, Sally reflected on the horrid details of Stephanie and her daughter's misadventures with Paul Alexander. "What were they thinking?" she said aloud while focusing on the car in front of her. "Now I gotta fix this mess."

When Cyrus Hampton was alive, the pact was tight and there were no loose ends. Eddie was the glue that held everyone together, and no one made a move unless there was a consensus. *Now look at Eddie. He's such a wimp. He has no control over anyone. We need order, and I plan on restoring it before we get in deeper trouble.*

Now that Cyrus Hampton was out of the picture, Sally zoomed in on Paul, who was standing in their way of freedom. Each member of the pact risked being indicted on charges involving grand larceny, fraud, and embezzlement. They could also potentially be sentenced up to twenty-five years in federal prison for their role.

As Sally pulled into her parking garage, she sat and thought about the weakest link. She figured Tameka might be the first to turn on all of them because she lacked self-confidence and grit. Unflinching and calculating, Sally determined she could not let that happen. She was determined to get rid of the weakest link before things got out of hand.

Chapter 40

Epiphany

Tameka was experiencing every stage of the battered women syndrome. She justified, coddled, and made excuses for her husband's verbal and mental abuse. Many times she questioned her sanity whenever Andy convinced her to believe his obvious lies. Divorce seemed inevitable. She was ready to give it all up.

After the meeting at the VFW club, she learned to release the stress caused by her broken marriage and her criminal involvement in the SCG embezzlement scheme. She returned home and parked her luxury Mercedes Benz in front of her five bedroom, four-bathroom home, which was immaculately landscaped with every exotic plant, tree, and flower imaginable. She acknowledged that her landscaper made her house the center of envy in the neighborhood.

Tameka reflected on her kids' private school even though they lived in Alexandria Virginia, which was known to have some of the best public schools in America. Then she focused on the pricey jewelry she purchased but did not need. Some of the most expensive pieces were missing but her husband convinced her that she had misplaced them. She also focused on all the other luxuries she possessed but the average person could not afford. *All these material things were acquired to please my husband. Now I'm taking my life back.*

After climbing out of her car, she walked up the long, curved path to the grand double door entrance. She opened the door and was pleasantly surprised when her kids ran into her arms. She embraced them as if it was the last time she would see them again. Tameka looked up at the babysitter and mouthed, "Thank you."

She paid the babysitter and told her that her services would no longer be necessary. Then she locked up her house and put the kids to bed. She waited until they closed their eyes before she went into her bedroom.

Sitting on her bed, Tameka was mentally preparing to make major changes in her life. She retrieved her cell phone from her purse to call her mother.

"I hope I didn't wake you," she said after her mother answered her call.

"I'm fine. Are you okay? You sound like something is troubling you."

"Mom, I need you to promise that you will take care of the kids…if something happens to me."

"What are you talking about?"

"Please promise me."

"Of course I will, but can you tell me what's going on?"

"I'm leaving Andy. I'm filing for a divorce."

"Good. I never liked him."

Tameka was at a loss for words. "I…didn't…know you felt that way about him."

"I pegged him as a shyster a long time ago. But I knew you were in-love. There is nothing I could have told you that would have convinced you not to marry him. I still can't get over the idea that you eloped. You're my only child, and I didn't get a chance to witness you getting married."

"I'm sorry."

"It's okay," her mom chuckled. "Maybe I can throw you a divorce party."

"Not where I'm going," Tameka mumbled under her breath.

"Honey, what did you say?"

"Uh…I'm going to see an attorney in the morning, but I need to send the kids to you after the school year ends, in two weeks. Are you sure you're able to keep the kids for me?"

"Don't be silly. Of course, I can. Are you sure you're okay?"

"Not really but I will be. I love you, Mom."

"I love you too."

When Tameka disconnected the call, she took a deep breath and exhaled. Her mind was at ease. She was ready to begin the next phase of her life.

Tameka made a mental note of things to do the next morning. *Call in to report absence from work, contact an attorney to file for a divorce, call a real estate agent to sell the house, withdraw what is left in the joint account, and set up a new account with her and her mother's name.*

More importantly, if Paul survived the abduction, meet with him to come clean about my role in the SCG investigation. Then call the FBI agent to finish responding to questions that stem from Cyrus Hampton's murder.

Satisfied with the list, Tameka took a shower and laid in bed. For the first time and a long time, she was able to go to sleep without dwelling on her problems. She slept like an angel.

Chapter 41

Monday Morning Blues

When Brian Jeffs reported to work as the new Deputy Director, his reception from some of the staff members was no different from Paul's. "Good morning," he said to everyone he passed in the hallway, but he did not get any responses. Instead, he got icy stares and daggers.

Further down the hallway, he noticed a middle-aged woman sitting at a desk in front of the Director's office. "That must be the Administrative Assistant," he said to himself as he approached her. "Uh...good morning, Ma'am."

Sally looked up from her computer and frowned. "What did you call me?"

"Huh?" Brian was perplexed by the question.

"Did you call me Ma'am?"

Brian held out his hand as if surrendering. "I'm sorry if I offended you. I didn't mean anything by it."

"Just so we are clear," she said in a firm tone, "my name is Sally Bates."

"Sorry, Ms. Bates...I didn't...."

"You can call me Sally," she countered with an attitude.

Brian shook his head and rolled his eyes upward when Sally resumed typing on the keyboard.

"How can I help you?" she asked, keeping her focus on the computer screen.

"My name is Brian Jeffs."

"I figured as much. Personnel told me you would be reporting to work today." Sally stood up, put on her sweater, and walked around her desk. "The Director is not in yet, so I'll show you to your office."

"Thank you."

Brian's office was next to Eddie's and across the aisle from Paul's. He walked into his new office and noticed the huge dark brown desk and leather high-back, office chair. He also spotted a small file cabinet next to the desk.

Sally waited for Brian to take it all in, before explaining, "Barrett Pike from the IT department will send someone to set up your computer and phone. In the meantime, follow me and I'll introduce you to the other deputy."

Like an obedient soldier, Brian followed the Administrative Assistant to his co-Deputy's office.

Eddie jumped up from his office chair as soon as Brian and Sally stepped in his office. He bore a wide, forced smile while approaching his new colleague with an extended hand. "You must be Brian Jeffs, our new deputy," he said, while vigorously shaking his hand.

Brian's brows scrunched inward while slowly removing his hand from Eddie's sweaty grasp. *So this is the butt-kisser Paul told me about.*

"Please have a seat." Eddie motioned for Brian to sit in the chair facing his desk. "Sally, you can leave now. Brian is in good hands."

Sally turned to Brian, and said, "Let me know if you need anything."

Over the next hour, Eddie explained the SCG process and political nature of the agency. He also took Brian around to introduce him to some SCG staff members. This time their disposition changed from icy-cold to thin smiles.

The IT Team Leader seemed stand-offish but pleasant toward the new deputy. Barrett told Brian that he sent someone to his office to install a new computer and phone. He also explained that he would get a technician to help Brian understand the automation tools and applications.

"That's good to know," Brian replied with a nod. "Will I get access to the SCG database?"

Barrett briefly glanced at Eddie, who appeared to freeze up. Then he turned his attention to Brian. "Uh…I don't see a problem with that. I'll work on getting you access."

"I'd appreciate that."

Next, Eddie introduced the new deputy to Stephanie. Unlike Barrett, she appeared to welcome Brian with open arms.

"Nice to meet you!" Stephanie enthusiastically greeted Brian with a robust hug. She held on to him a little longer than necessary and only released him after lightly squeezing his buttocks.

"It's nice…to meet you too." Brian was caught off guard by Stephanie's display of affection. He thought it was odd when she rubbed her breasts against his chest during the embrace.

Eddie stood back and looked at her in disbelief. He had known Stephanie a long time and knew she was over dramatizing her meeting with Brian. He made a mental note to tell her to chill out.

"So," Eddie said to break up the awkward greeting, "let me introduce you to the HR staff. Tameka Collins-Brown is the Team Leader, who is responsible for signing off on most of our SCG projects."

"But she's not in yet," Stephanie volunteered. She had looked at the electronic sign-in sheet earlier and noticed Tameka did not sign in.

"Oh...that's too bad." Eddie was clearly perplexed. "Do you know if she will be reporting to work today?"

Stephanie shrugged. Then she retrieved her cell phone from her purse. "I'll give her a call to find out."

"I'd appreciate that. I'm going to take Brian to Personnel to introduce him to staff."

Eddie began to walk away with Brian on his heels. Then he suddenly turned back to Stephanie. "Make sure you tell me if you are able to contact Tameka."

"I will," Stephanie said while holding the phone to her ear. She left a message after her call was directed to Tameka's voicemail.

***

Brian could not wait to return to his new office. He sat in his chair, threw his hands up, and mouthed, "I made it!" All my hard work paid off. Thanks to my buddy, for looking out." Which reminds me," he said as he retrieved his cell phone from his suit pocket to call Paul.

"Hello," Paul answered.

"You sound wide awake. You were still sleep when I left the house this morning."

"I was exhausted. I suppose this is how it feels after you've been kidnapped and rescued."

They both fell over from laughter.

"So Paul," Brian said after regaining his composure, "what are you up to today?"

"I'm on my way to DC to meet with Jimmy, the President's adviser. How are things going on your first day at SCG?"

"Sally is a trip."

Paul chuckled. "Give her some time. She'll warm up to you."

"Yeah, okay." Brian was not convinced.

"Anything else going on?"

"I met most of the staff today, except the HR Team Leader. She hasn't reported to work yet."

"That's strange. Tameka is normally an early person."

"And that Stephanie McPherson is weird."

"What makes you think that?"

"That broad gave me a bodacious hug and grabbed my behind when she introduced herself. I felt like I was groped by an old Aunt."

Paul cracked a smile. "That's odd. I never thought of her as the frisky type."

"Definitely not my cup of tea. Oh…before I forget. I met Barrett Pike today. He told me he's going to get me access to the SCG database."

"Good luck with that. He stalled on getting me access, and when he finally did – I've been bombarded with error messages ever since."

"Do you think it's intentional?"

"I'm not sure. I only know one person that can get pass the bugs."

"Don't mention his name," Brian warned.

"I know your brother is a scrounger, but he's sharp and smart. I may need his expertise."

"I'll think about it. Will I see you when I get home?"

"That depends on my meeting at the White House. I'll call you later."

After Brian disconnected the call, he thought about his brother, Charlie. Paul was right about his brother's intelligence. When he graduated from high school, Charlie attended the Palm Beach IT school. He was a fast learner. In less than six months of attending the school, he was offered a job as the school's computer lab technician.

Charlie was even in the local newspaper for reversing a hack job done on the Palm Beach County public school system. The children were unable to obtain the schedules to start classes, because the school was blocked from updating their records. Charlie was sent to the rescue after the school board reached out to the IT school for assistance.

With newfound notoriety, several organizations started reaching out to Charlie to fix their complex IT issues. The pressure from becoming one of the most sought-after IT experts became too much for him. He became a recluse. Then he started drinking and found it difficult to rebound.

Chapter 42

Second Wind

Tameka had gotten a late start when she woke up the next morning. After oversleeping, she rushed to feed the kids breakfast and get them to school. Then she started working on her to-do list but in no particular order.

The bank was in her vicinity, so she drove there first to open a new bank account. Tameka was shocked when she arrived at the bank and the teller told her she had a negative balance.

"Are you sure?" she asked the teller.

"Yes, over ten thousand dollars was withdrawn from the account two days ago."

"Whha....what!" Tameka could barely contain herself. In addition to her net paycheck, the ten thousand dollars in the joint account was just enough to cover all of their bills for the next two months. She was livid.

The teller looked at the monitor before explaining, "Andrew Brown is listed as the co-owner of this account. Our records show he withdrew the money."

Tameka started shaking her head vigorously. "Andy wouldn't do this to me."

"I can show you a copy of the withdrawal slip, but it is also available online."

"Please...print...it...out for me. I need to see it now." Tameka's voice was shaking. She rested her elbows on the counter and rubbed her forehead with her forefingers. She was trying to do everything in her power to remain in control.

She nearly lost it when the teller showed her the printout of the withdrawal slip with Andy's signature. Tameka broke out in tears.

"Mrs. Brown," the teller said as she rested her hand on Tameka's shoulder. "I want to tell you something but I can lose my job if you share this information with anyone."

Tameka wiped away her tears with the back of her hand and nodded in understanding. "I promise...if you can help me...I swear...."

"I believe you." The teller leaned over and explained in a hushed tone, "Your husband has another bank account that solely bears his name."

"Are you serious?" Tameka bawled and started crying hysterically.

"Mrs. Brown, I believe there's a way you can get your money back."

"How?" Tameka asked, after sniffling and drying her tears from the tissue the teller provided her.

"Online. Do you have the USER ID and pin number for your joint account?"

"Yes."

"It's a hunch but it's possible that your husband uses the same USER ID and pin number for his account."

"Do you really believe that?" Tameka's question was filled with doubt.

The teller smiled as she slid a piece of paper with Andy's new account number on it. "There's only one way to find out. Find a computer or use your cell phone to do a little digging."

Tameka mouthed, "Thank you," before she pulled out her cell phone and turned to leave. She sat in her car in the bank parking lot to access the account online. A prompt asked her to verify Andy's identity by email or text. Tameka selected the email option because she knew her husband's credentials. Besides, the text option would have alerted him that she was attempting to access his account.

Within seconds, the bank sent a six-digit pin to Andy's email address. Tameka's eyes popped out of her head when she used the username and PIN number to their joint account and the verification code that was sent to Andy's email to access his bank account. Their joint account with the negative balance was also listed as one of his accounts.

Andy had more than one-hundred thousand dollars in his bank account. Tameka viewed the credit and debit transactions and noticed that most of the withdrawals from the joint account matched the deposits in his account. Andy had been siphoning money from their joint account and transferring the money to his account for the past six months.

Tameka slammed her fist on the steering wheel, and shouted, "*That son of a bitch! I will show him.*" She allowed her fingers to do the talking when she transferred all except one dollar from her husband's bank account back to their joint account. Then she went into the bank and greeted the same teller that supplied her with Andy's new bank account information.

The teller smiled when she noticed the big grin on Tameka's face. "I take it you want to withdraw the money from your joint account today and open another account at a different bank. Am I correct?"

Tameka nodded. "I can't thank you enough."

"I'm happy to oblige." The teller completed the transaction and handed Tameka a bulky envelope filled with a hundred one-thousand-dollar bills. "Enjoy your new life."

Tameka smiled. "Thanks to you."

The teller nodded in understanding.

Tameka turned to leave as she recalled the teller's last words. *Enjoy your new life*. The magnitude of those words hit her like a ton of bricks. She broke down crying again before pulling herself together.

When she climbed in her car, she noticed a missed call from her co-worker, Stephanie. She thought about returning the call, but only for a fleeting moment. Revisiting the list of things to do, she contacted the local real estate agent to put the house up for sale. She explained that she wanted the house to be listed 'As Is,' including all the furniture.

"Are you sure?" the real estate agent inquired. "What about your husband?"

"The house is solely in my name."

"But the state of Maryland is a 50/50 State. What if your husband contests the transaction?"

"Don't worry, he won't. How soon can you list the house for sale?"

"I need my photographer to take some pictures first, but we can have it on the market right away."

"Sounds like a plan."

"This is a seller's market so we shouldn't have a problem selling your home in an efficient manner."

"Good. I have some errands to run, but I'll be home in a couple of hours."

Tameka checked her watch after disconnecting the call. She called the HR department and told her Assistant that she would not be reporting to work. She explained that she was taking care of a family emergency.

Chapter 43

DAMN!!!!

After Brian Jeffs returned to his office, Eddie spotted Stephanie in the hallway making copies of newly created evidentiary documents. He approached to her to inquire about her loose and flirty disposition with the man that happened to share his job title.

"What was that all about?" he asked through slanted eyes.

Stephanie chuckled. "I was just toying with our new deputy, that's all.

"We don't want to do anything to bring attention to ourselves. So stop doing whatever you're trying to do."

"Lighten up, Eddie," she replied with a sly grin and shrugged shoulders. "Why are you so defensive? The way I see it, you are the one that should be worried."

"What are you saying?"

"I can only think of one reason why Paul Alexander hired Brian Jeffs."

"And what reason would that be?"

"To replace you." Stephanie shook her head in disgust. "You should have done more to shut down the Director's probe. Now we could all be in jeopardy because of you."

"You can't blame me for this. I didn't put a gun to your head and force you to create fake pensioners. This was all your brilliant idea. I am the accessory to your scheme but this was all on you."

"Let's not forget that you benefited from my scheme!" Her voice was so loud, anyone within earshot could have heard her.

Eddie looked around for fear Stephanie's voice would draw unwanted attention. Then he turned to her and waved his hands downward. "Let's calm down. This is not the place to discuss this."

"I can't afford to go to prison," Stephanie admitted in a hushed whisper. "My girls need me."

"No one is going to jail. The Director doesn't know anything."

"Are you sure?"

"Yes, the IT Team Leader is making sure Paul cannot access the information he needs. As far as I'm concerned, the Director's investigation is stymied without evidence."

"I hope you're right." Stephanie was overcome with uneasiness as she turned to go to her office.

Eddie was also feeling doubtful about the situation. The Director had been keeping him locked out of the investigation since day one. Now he had to deal with Brian Jeffs, which was a mystery to everyone, especially to Eddie. He wondered if Paul hired the new deputy to spy on them. But he needed to know for sure. Mentally, he devised a plan to elicit answers from his Co-Deputy.

Chapter 44

R-E-S-P-E-C-T

Continuing with the to-do list, Tameka contacted her attorney to handle her and her husband's assets and dissolve their marriage. She made it clear to the attorney that she did not want anything to do with the hotel in the Virgin Islands. The only thing she wanted was for Andy to pay child support for their kids.

The attorney insisted that she would not have a problem selling the house without her husband's consent, since the house was solely in her name. He explained that she and her husband signed a post-nuptial agreement so she would not have problems keeping the proceeds from the sale of the house.

"So he only needs to sign the petition for dissolution of marriage form, and our marriage will be over," Tameka stated to be sure.

"Basically. That is, unless you want to resolve the child support arrangements beforehand."

"No, I can wait until after the divorce."

"If that's the case, your divorce will be finalized within thirty days after I receive the signed form from your husband. But the electronic signature would expedite the process."

"Great. You can send the form to my email address, and I'll text you my husband's email address."

"I'll contact you as soon as I receive the e-signature for you and your husband on the dissolution of marriage form."

"Thank you."

Tameka sent the attorney a text with Andy's email address after disconnecting the call. She took a deep breath and prayed for strength before making the next call.

"How are you?" she asked, after Andy answered her call on the third ring. She sounded nice but her question was riddled with cynicism.

"Hey, baby. I miss you already," Andy replied in-kind, but it came across as forced and fake.

"I'm sure you do." Tameka rolled her eyes, before explaining, "You missed me so much that you left your family penniless."

"Uh…what…."

"I know what you did to our joint bank account."

"I can explain. You see, uh…the hotel needed some repairs…and…."

"Bullshit!" Tameka fired back. "You should check your account. I left you plenty of money to survive."

"What are you saying?"

"The attorney is preparing a petition for our divorce. He's going to send it to you via email. I need you to sign it electronically and return it as soon as you receive it."

"Let's not be hasty. Let me explain."

"No!" Tameka snapped. "You are to listen to me! When you insisted that we sign a post-nuptial agreement, I was concerned that it meant you would leave me penniless. I was right, Andy. The best part of the agreement is that you insisted that I put the house solely in my name. You also insisted that I keep the house in case we get a divorce. I have nothing but RESPECT for your wise decision."

"What are you saying?"

"The negative balance you left in our joint account told me all I needed to know about you and your intentions for this family. Luckily for me, I found your new account information. I was able to transfer all except one dollar back to our joint account."

"Good," Andy said. "I shouldn't have done that to you. I don't know what I was thinking."

"But I do, which is why I closed our joint account and deposited the money in a new account at a different bank. But I'm willing to return half of it, if you sign the dissolution of marriage petition and return it the same day."

"How can I be certain you will return the money to my bank account?"

"You just have to trust me." Tameka had already decided to return some of the money but not fifty percent.

"What about our kids?" Andy inquired in a winy voice.

"What about them? They barely know you. When you are home, you don't even spend time with them. You are a sorry excuse for a father."

"You can't take my kids from me."

"I would never do that. If you're interested in seeing the kids, you should file the necessary paperwork through court for visitation rights."

"I don't understand why you're doing this," Andy said out of frustration. Then his demeanor changed. "Tameka, you don't want to fuck with me. I can make your life miserable."

"If you are talking about the SCG investigation, think again. I plan on coming clean, and I'll deal with the consequences."

Andy opened his mouth to speak but closed it after realizing he did not have a proper response.

"What's the matter? The cat got your tongue. I hope you and your mistress rot in hell!" On that note, Tameka disconnected the call. She felt like patting herself on back, after standing up to her husband for the first and only time.

Chapter 45

Life Before Death

Almost a year before his death, Cyrus Hampton had initiated an investigation to explore the possibility of fraud at SCG. He believed something was amiss after noticing an uptick in the number of newly created identities established by SCG, compared to prior years. However, annual audits did not show anything out of the ordinary.

Accepting the results from the most recent audit was Cyrus' only recourse. That was, until he had an affair with his Administrative Assistant. Cyrus and Sally Bates started seeing each other in intimate settings soon after her husband died. He had attended her husband's funeral and was there to comfort her while she was in mourning.

One night he had visited her home after she did not respond to his many phone calls. He found her sitting on the bench on her porch, staring into space. "Are you okay?" he asked as he slowly approached her. "I tried calling but you did not return my messages."

She looked up at him and nodded. "I'll be okay. I'm just having a hard time dealing with being alone."

"Is there anything I can do for you?"

Sally opened her mouth but closed it to measure her words. Then she admitted in a soft-spoken voice, "This may sound inappropriate, but I need to be held. I miss the way my husband...." Her voice trailed off after she started weeping and struggling to say more.

Cyrus walked onto her porch, sat on the bench, and embraced her. "It's going to be okay," he said in soothing words.

Sally nodded after drying her tears with her hands.

Cyrus smiled and looked into her eyes. "I'm here for you whenever you need me."

In response, she stared into his sparkly, bright eyes. Then she leaned toward him and planted a kiss on his lips.

Realizing things had gotten out of hand, Cyrus hurriedly pulled away from her and stood up. "I'm sorry if I misled you. I'm married for God's sake!"

"You didn't mislead me. I just wanted to feel the same thing I felt when my husband was alive."

"I understand. But you are my subordinate."

Sally shook her head as if she were shaking away the truth about their professional relationship. "I won't apologize," she admitted after she stood up and faced him. "For few seconds, you made me feel as if I could love again."

Blushing and feeling gushy inside, no one including his wife had ever told Cyrus that he made them feel that way. He looked at her face and thought she was breathtakingly beautiful without makeup. Suddenly, he felt conflicted and weak at the knees.

Sally smiled and lightly patted his chest. "Don't worry about me. I'll be fine. Go on home."

"Do you think you will return to work soon?"

She nodded. "More than likely."

That day set off a one-month affair that Sally and Cyrus had never predicted. They both needed each other, and both wanted to be desired.

Cyrus' wife was always out of town visiting her sick mother, which made it easier for him to see Sally at a minute's notice. Besides, Cyrus believed his wife had checked out of their marriage after her mother's health deteriorated.

But the relationship with Sally took a turn for the worse. Cyrus learned that Sally drank alcohol excessively. It was during those moments she would reminisce about her deceased husband. It was not often that she overindulged but when it happened, she would reveal intriguing secrets.

During one of his overnight stays with Sally, she started drinking and slurring her words. His ears perked up, when she said, "I wonder how much...they're getting from...SCG accounts." Sally burped after continuing with incoherent rambling. "As long as...they give me...money...."

"What are you talking about?" Cyrus questioned, hoping she would divulge specifics.

"You...know...."

Cyrus shook his head. "Why don't you tell me?"

Sally put two fingers together over her lips, and whispered, "Shhhhhhhh.... It's a secret."

"Who's involved?"

Sally started waving her head back and forth before she burst out in laughter.

Cyrus tried nudging her shoulders to get her to focus. "Talk to me," he insisted. "What about the accounts?"

Sally smiled and said in a wicked voice, "I know…what you…don't know." She grinned before she stretched out on the sofa and closed her eyes.

Cyrus tried to nudge her awake but it did not work. He became exasperated after Sally drifted off to sleep. He retrieved a blanket from the linen closet and laid it across her body. Then he turned off the lights, locked the front door, and headed home.

Restless and shaken, Cyrus stayed up most of the night. He had gleaned from Sally that his employees were possibly committing fraud. He looked forward to talking with her the next day, with the hope of obtaining additional information.

***

Sally had promptly showed up at work the next morning. She was feeling rejuvenated after recovering from her drunken stupor. A smile spread across her face when she spotted the Director getting off the elevator. But she grew concerned after he approached her desk with furrowed brows and a sharp gaze.

"What's the matter with you, Cyrus?"

"Sally, I need to talk to you in my office. You don't need a pen and pad."

After nodding, she followed Cyrus into his office and sat across from his desk. She listened as her Director recited everything she had muttered while she was drunk.

"What do you know, Sally? Is something going on at SCG that I'm not aware of?"

"I don't know what you're talking about," Sally spoke softly under her breath.

"I believe you do. I need to know if any SCG staff members are making money from establishing accounts."

"I'm sorry…I can't help you."

"Are you involved?"

"I can't do this." Sally stood up and sighed. "I think it's best that we do not see each other anymore."

"Is that what you want?"

"I think it's for the best."

Sally left the office and closed the door behind her. From that day forward, she and Cyrus had maintained a professional relationship. Their friendship was unmistakably broken.

Chapter 46

Missing Link

Cyrus Hampton realized Sally Bates would not provide him information he desperately needed. Unsettled with her lack of cooperation and the findings from the most recent audit, Cyrus launched a formal investigation at SCG. He had interviewed several SCG staff, but he was not able to gather any information that would confirm or negate the possibility of fraud.

A breakthrough occurred when he spotted a file on Tameka Collins-Brown desk. After searching through the file, he noticed Stephanie McPherson created the new account. The turn-around period to establish new identities for SCG clients was normally two weeks, but the file had been sitting on Tameka's desk for almost a month. *What about the customer?* he thought to himself. *His life could be in danger without a new identity and evidentiary documents. Something isn't right.*

Cyrus had a hunch about the file, its contents, and Tameka's possible involvement. He retrieved the file from her desk and headed to his office. Then he made arrangements to meet with her. Instead of questioning Tameka about the file, he thought he would try a different tactic.

As soon as Tameka arrived at his office, Cyrus showed her the file that he found on her desk. Then he looked closely into her eyes and watched her slump in the chair. "Tameka," he began in an accusatory tone, "someone recently notified me that staff are committing fraud here at SCG. Tell me about your involvement."

Tameka's eyes popped out of her head, before she started stuttering, "I...don't...know what...you are talking about."

Cyrus bit his bottom lip to restrain from telling her he believed she was lying. "Tell me what you know," he persisted.

Casting her eyes downward, Tameka mumbled under her breath, "I may know something, but I can't talk about it."

"Are you involved?"

She nodded, avoiding eye contact.

Cyrus told her about the ramifications of committing fraud, including difficulties of not being able to see her children if she were thrown in prison.

After checking the calendar on his desk, he told Tameka that he would give her until the next business day to come clean about everything she knew. He figured she would have all weekend to mull over her decision. Otherwise, he would have no choice but to escalate the matter.

He had meant to scare her into coming clean, but something was holding her back. He did not realize the extent of her involvement, or whether her life was possibly in jeopardy.

***

Prior to meeting Tameka, Cyrus had contacted Barrett Pike to obtain a computer printout of the new identities. The printout would have revealed who created the accounts for the past year. He became exasperated when the IT Team Leader kept delaying his requests.

It did not help that his deputy created roadblocks that made it improbable for him to obtain the information he needed. All Eddie provided him were assurances that there was no fraudulent activity at SCG. But Cyrus was not convinced.

He had called the President of the United States to report that he had initiated an investigation. He had explained his efforts so far, had not yielded any results.

The President asked, "Do you want me to send the FBI to investigate?"

"No, not right now," Cyrus countered. "I may have an employee that's willing to talk. I will let you know by Monday whether we should notify the FBI."

"Cyrus, this would be embarrassing if this fraud scheme is taking place on my watch. I want to nip this in the bud without fanfare from news reporters."

"I promise. I'll do everything in my power to keep this investigation under wraps."

"I'd appreciate it. Keep me posted on your progress."

After the call with the President, Cyrus had ordered his deputy to his office. For the first time, he had explained to Eddie what he had learned from Sally Bates. He was careful not to reveal her name.

Suddenly, he realized he never interviewed his deputy. So he asked, "Are you sure you don't know anything?"

"I can assure you," Eddie replied with confidence, "that you would be the first to know – if anything is going on at SCG. We are audited every five years, and our records are always spotless. In fact, the recent audit did not reveal any fraudulent activities."

Cyrus nodded in agreement. "I suppose you're right. But let me know if you hear anything. In the meantime, I have some leads that I'm going to follow up on."

"You do?" Eddie asked with raised brows. "Can you tell me about your leads?"

Cyrus hesitated before responding to Eddie. He realized that his deputy could be a potential suspect. Revealing the evidence he stored in his safe could hamper the investigation.

"No," Cyrus finally said. "This is something I have to work on independently. The President is relying on my expertise to ensure that we mitigate any possibility of fraud."

Eddie's mouth flew open from shock. "You mean Madam President Elizabeth Sanchez Varona?"

"Yes, who else would I be referring to?"

"You told the President about the SCG investigation?"

"Of course, she is my boss." Cyrus frowned and tilted his head, before asking, "What's up with the dozen questions?"

"I'm just surprised, that's all. Is there anything else you need?"

"No, that'll be all."

Cyrus figured that if he could not get the printout of the new identities, he would retain newly created evidentiary documents that were supposed to be released to the various government agencies for their records. He had collected the documents over a two-week period and stored them in the safe in his office.

Typically, he would review the evidentiary documents and sign off for their release. He figured he would use the documents to determine if the new identities were legitimate. He also wanted to explore if there were pensioners associated with the new identities.

Cyrus was cognizant that spy agents with a new identity did not want to be found. He also realized the process of elimination, to determine who was legit was a long shot but worth a try.

After careful thought, he called a personal friend of his that happened to work for the Central Intelligence Agency. "I need a favor," he said after the CIA Officer answered his call.

"What's going on?"

Cyrus had explained the purpose and status of the SCG investigation in less than fifteen minutes. Then he asked, "Can you find out if any pensioners are associated with these documents?"

"Yes, I can do that for you. How many?"

"I have eleven distinct evidentiary documents in my possession."

"Cyrus, I must be honest with you. It may be difficult to locate all the spy agents since you have the evidence in your possession. But I may have luck if the agents are receiving a pension."

"How long will it take for you to locate them?"

"Give me a week or two. Send me copies of the documents."

"I'll fax them to you today." Cyrus paused before commenting, "I'd appreciate it if you keep this between us."

"I understand. You have my word."

After disconnecting the call, Cyrus faxed copies of the documents to his friend at the CIA. Then he returned the items to the safe in his office. The file he had retrieved from Tameka's desk was never processed, so he had asked his Administrative Assistant to file it in Archives.

Satisfied with his decisions relating to the investigation, Cyrus grabbed his suit jacket and briefcase before exiting his office. He looked forward to going home to relax and possibly watch a basketball game on his sixty-five-inch TV.

Chapter 47

Day of Reckoning

Upon arriving home, Cyrus Hampton parked his car in front of the garage and walked down to the mailbox to retrieve the mail. Then he strolled up the path to the front door to enter his home. The house was quiet as usual. He assumed his wife was out of town again, visiting her elderly mother, who was lucid and in a nursing home in Florida.

When he entered his home, he locked the front door and went into the kitchen to get a bite to eat. He opened the refrigerator and noticed a freshly made shake in a ninja smoothie cup, which was encapsulated with a matching lid. Affixed to the cup, was a yellow sticky note that read: *"Sorry I couldn't make dinner. Enjoy the smoothie. Will call when I get to Florida."*

Cyrus was surprised by his wife's gesture, especially since she stopped making dinner for them two years earlier, the same time she started visiting her mother in Florida. So the smoothie was a big shocker.

After removing the smoothie from the refrigerator, Cyrus decided not to question her thoughtfulness. He gulped a large portion of the fruity but grainy smoothie. When his stomach grumbled, he sat the smoothie cup on the countertop to retrieve a frozen dinner out of the freezer. With a knife, he put small slits in the plastic portion of the dinner for ventilation. Then he put the dinner in the microwave, turned on the timer, and sat in the stool in front of the countertop.

Eagerly, he resumed drinking the smoothie. He thought it was too sweet but he couldn't resist the taste of fresh berries. He made a mental note to thank his wife.

The microwave alerted him that his meal was complete. His legs wobbled when he stood up. Suddenly, he felt a sharp pain in his heart and the smoothie cup fell out of his hand and onto the floor. Cyrus could not think straight. His vision became blurry and he could not find his cell phone. He tried to holler for help but the lack of oxygen in his lungs seemed to strangle him.

Crawling like a turtle was the only way he could function. He made it to the front door and was able to turn the doorknob. Sweat was protruding down his face and his heart was beating rapidly, as he shimmied out the front door and onto the porch.

"Help!" Cyrus screamed but could not hear his voice. He managed to crawl down the steps and onto the path leading to the sidewalk in front of his home. All of a sudden, his heartbeat slowed and became irregular. He could not move.

Ten minutes later, his neighbor arrived home and found him stretched out in the pathway leading to the front of his house. The young man rushed to Cyrus' aid but noticed the situation was quickly deteriorating. The frantic neighbor called 911 to report Cyrus was having a heart-attack. By the time the ambulance arrived, his body went limp and he had stopped breathing.

***

Cyrus did not know he was not alone in his house. An uninvited visitor had witnessed his demise from his living room window.

When the ambulance arrived, the visitor walked into the kitchen with black gloves to retrieve the note that was affixed to the smoothie cup. Then the visitor slipped through the back door and into the backyard, which was surrounded by an overgrown conservation easement.

Traversing through the heavily wooded area, the visitor arrived at the main road, where they had initially parked their getaway car. The road was dimly lit and void of cars. So the mysterious person was able to escape the area without being detected.

Chapter 48

Let There Be Light

When Paul arrived at the White House, he met with the President's Senior Advisor, Jimmy Johnson. Paul told the advisor about his progress on the SCG investigation and the roadblocks he had encountered to obtain evidence of potential fraud. Then he presented the evidentiary documents he had retrieved from the safe in his office.

Jimmy looked at the evidence as if he had seen it already. "I have a phone call to make," he said as he retrieved his cell phone from his suit pocket to contact the White House receptionist. He told her he was ready to receive the visitor. "Make sure you send him to the main conference room," he added before disconnecting the call.

"What's going on?" Paul inquired.

"I believe this evidence is why a CIA Officer is waiting in our reception area."

"Come again?"

"The FBI stated a CIA Officer had reached out to them after Cyrus Hampton was murdered."

"Why?"

"I believe the officer possesses evidence similar to what you are presenting today."

Paul frowned. "I'm confused."

"Evidently, Cyrus Hampton shared the evidence with a CIA Officer before he was murdered."

"Why didn't I know about this?"

"We were just as blindsided as you. Cyrus was conducting a secret operation without the proper protocol. I asked the CIA Officer to meet with me today to share what he knows."

When Secret Service escorted the CIA Officer to the conference room, Jimmy Johnson shook his hand and introduced him to the SCG Director. In response, Paul stood up, and said, "I'm glad you are here." He shook the young man's hand with a firm grip.

"Please have a seat," Jimmy told the young man. "Did you bring the evidence you have in your possession?"

"Sir, I don't have the actual evidence but I do have facsimiles." The Officer provided a large envelope with the documents to Jimmy.

Jimmy perused through the documents before handing them over to Paul.

Paul looked at the documents and noticed they were copies of evidence in his possession. Then he asked the Officer, "Why did Cyrus Hampton send you these documents?"

"Cyrus asked me to investigate whether the new identities established from the evidentiary documents are legitimate. He also wanted me to verify if there are any pensioners associated with the new identities."

"And what did you discover?" Paul asked.

"From the evidentiary documents Cyrus Hampton faxed to me, I was able to verify that the new identities of five individuals are legitimate. Three of the individuals are pensioners who have retirement benefits direct deposited into their bank accounts on a monthly basis. It's safe to assume that the other two individuals established bank accounts to receive payments for contracted jobs."

Paul and Jimmy nodded in understanding. They were aware that spy agents receive compensation for every job they complete.

"What about the new identities associated with the other documents?" Paul asked.

"I could not verify the legitimacy of new identities issued for individuals listed on the remaining documents. However, Treasury confirmed that five of the individuals receive retirement benefits and the monthly checks are direct deposited to online bank accounts."

Paul frowned, before stating, "There are eleven evidentiary documents, but you only accounted for ten."

"There is a passport, but the Department of State confirmed it has not been used. Also, Treasury confirmed that there is no bank account information listed for this individual."

Paul sighed. "SCG is supposed to be the most discrete federal government agency in the country. There are cracks in the system if you found a way to locate some of the spy agents."

"Not necessarily," the Officer countered. "I could not have located them without the documents."

Jimmy nodded before asking, "How did you verify the identity of five of the individuals without making direct contact with them?"

"I followed the money. My contact at Treasury extracted the physical addresses from the national direct deposit system.

I was able to get a match after plugging in the addresses into various government databases."

Paul sat on the edge of his chair, before asking, "What about the other individuals? Were you able to get their addresses?"

The CIA Officer nodded. "Yes, but I was unable to locate the names listed on the evidentiary documents with the addresses supplied by Treasury."

"Do you know whose names are associated with the addresses?"

"There were P O Box addresses listed in the national direct deposit system. But my contact at the U.S. Postal Service located names and residential addresses of three SCG staff members."

In that instance, Jimmy stood up. "Why are we still here? We have to get warrants and arrest everyone involved in creating fake identities and embezzling government funds."

"Have a seat, Jimmy," Paul interjected. "I don't think it's that simple. We do not have proof that SCG staff created fake identities or received pension funds. Circumstantial evidence is not enough for a conviction."

"You're right," Jimmy said as he sat back down in his seat. "But the Officer stated he has the bank information for all the pensioners."

"Yeah," the CIA Officer interjected, "but the names on the bank accounts do not match the names of the SCG staff members."

"What do you suggest?" Jimmy asked Paul.

"Gaining access to the SCG database will tell us who created the fake identities. I know someone that can help us."

"Does this person work for the government?"

"No he doesn't. But hiring this person for the job will eliminate the red tape."

Jimmy thought about the lengthy process it would take for the NSA to hack into the database. "Okay," he said after pondering the urgency of the matter, "hire the guy and I'll get you the money to pay him. But are you sure it's wise to sit on this evidence without at least requesting warrants?"

"Give me some time to follow-up on some leads. I'll be in touch."

Chapter 49

Breakthrough...

When Paul left the White House, he headed to the Select Committee for General Services building in Alexandria, Virginia. He wanted to brief his new deputy about the status of the SCG investigation. He also wanted to discuss the possibility of hiring Brian Jeff's brother for a hack job.

Suddenly, his cell phone rang as he headed northbound on I-295. He glanced at the Caller ID and noticed it was an unknown number. He hesitated before he answered the call. "Who is this?"

"Tameka Collins-Brown. Is this Paul Alexander?" she asked to be sure. She recalled Stephanie's story about kidnapping him and leaving him for dead.

"Yes, this is me. Where are you?"

"I'm home waiting for my real estate agent."

Paul's brows furrowed, after wondering if Tameka was trying to avoid a likely conviction. "Are you moving?"

"Something like that. I'm ready to talk."

"Text me your address now," he said in a blunt tone, "and you better be there when I get there."

"I'll be here. You will receive my text in a few seconds."

After disconnecting the call, Paul called Brian Jeff's cell phone but did not get an answer. He left a message that he needed to discuss an urgent matter. He also called his friend's office number but Sally, the Administrative Assistant, told him Brian was not in his office.

"Is he out to lunch?" Paul asked out of curiosity.

"I believe so. He left the office a little while ago with Eddie."

"Okay, thanks for letting me know."

"Is there anything I can do to help you?" Sally asked, hoping to get specifics.

"No, I'm good. Thank you for asking, though."

"Paul, I didn't know you had an offsite meeting. Nothing is on your calendar."

Paul chuckled to himself. He never told Sally he was attending a meeting offsite. "Sorry about that," he coyly replied. "The meeting was unexpected. I'll make sure to keep you posted in the future."

"Paul, I have some errands to run. I'll be leaving early today."

"That's not a problem. Have a nice evening."

After disconnecting the call, Sally hurriedly grabbed her purse to leave the office. She had been thinking about the weakest link for a while. Up for the task, she wanted to make sure Tameka kept her mouth shut.

Chapter 50

The Untangling

Paul drove up Tameka's massive driveway and was instantly in awe of the beautiful landscaping. The exterior of the six thousand square-foot home was also breathtaking. Though the beauty of her home was overshadowed by the *For Sale* sign.

Tameka opened the front door as soon as Paul stepped on to the porch. "Please come in," she said in a soft whisper.

"Why is your house up for sale?"

"Let's just say, 'I'm cleaning house.'" Tameka pointed to the chair in the living room. "You can have a seat."

"You said you were ready to talk," Paul said as he unbuttoned his suit jacket and sat on the edge of the chair.

"Yes, I just need time to get some things in order before I send my kids to live with my mother in North Carolina. She agreed to take care of them for me."

Paul nodded in understanding. "Tell me what you know."

"I am responsible for providing the first sign off on all pensioners, including the fake ones."

"Are you acting alone?"

"No."

"Who else is involved?"

Tameka hesitated. She wasn't sure if she should name her accomplices. "I need protection if I tell you. I can't put my family in danger."

"What makes you think you will be in danger?"

"They killed Cyrus Hampton and I heard that you were kidnapped."

Paul flashed back to the time he was kidnapped and left for dead in Pennsylvania. "Do you know who kidnapped me?"

Tameka nodded.

"I can get you immunity if you become a witness for the Federal Prosecutor. I can also assist with getting you and your family in the Witness Protection Program. But you have to come clean with everything you know."

"I understand."

"Does your husband know about your involvement?"

"Only that I benefited from some of the fake pensioners. But you don't have to worry about him. I filed for a divorce which should be final in 30 days. I'm tired," she admitted, before bursting out in tears. "I wanted to stop but they wouldn't let me."

"Who is they?" Paul tried to egg her on but Tameka's face was riddled with fear. He sensed that she was at a breaking point. He looked at the picture on the wall above the living room sofa and noticed the young boy and twin girls. Paul's heart melted at the thought of the children living the rest of their childhood without their mother. He wanted to help Tameka.

"Pack up as much as you can. I'm going to make a phone call to get you and your children admitted into the Witness Protection program today."

"Thank you," Tameka whispered with tears flooding down her face.

"We still need a statement from you explaining the fraud and everyone involved. Do you understand?"

Tameka nodded while wiping her tears with the back of her hand. Then she stood up and slowly made it upstairs to pack their things.

As soon as Tameka disappeared from sight, Paul retrieved his cell phone from his suit pocket and called the President's Senior Advisor.

"Jimmy, I'm here with an SCG employee, Tameka Collins-Brown. She needs to be admitted in the Witness Protection program, pronto. She agreed to give a complete statement of her participation in the SCG embezzlement scheme and provide the names of everyone involved."

"That's good to hear. Send me her address. I will send the U.S. Marshalls to take her statement and retrieve Mrs. Collins and her family within an hour."

"There is no husband," Paul explained. "It'll be just the mother and three kids."

Thirty minutes later, five undercover cars converged on Tameka's property. The U.S. Marshalls cornered off her property while Tameka rushed around her house to get the most vital things for her and her children. Then she sat with Paul and two U.S. Marshalls to give her statement on the SCG scheme.

One of the agents explained that she will be disconnected from her family and friends until the case was over.

"What about my mother?" Tameka inquired. "She lives alone and I worry that her life could also be in jeopardy."

The agent glanced at Paul who gave his approval with a nod. "You need to call your mother and tell her to gather as much as she can. We can send an agent to retrieve her within an hour."

"Thank you," Tameka said with relief.

Paul said, "You're not out of the woods yet. I'm still working on getting you immunity."

"I know. I'm ready to deal with the consequences of my actions."

"Good for you. I have to leave now, but you're in good hands."

Chapter 51

See ~~No~~ Evil

As Paul drove away from Tameka's home, he noticed a woman parked a half-block away. She looked eerily familiar to him. Then it dawned on him that it was none other than his Administrative Assistant. *What in the hell is Sally doing here? And why is she sitting in the car down the street from where Tameka lives?*

Suddenly, it dawned on Paul that Tameka had listed the Administrative Assistant as a suspect in the SCG scheme. He did not know what Sally's intentions were, but he did not want to take a chance that she will tell the others about what she likely witnessed at Tameka's home.

Paul called Jimmy, the President's Senior Advisor, to arrange to have Sally arrested on the spot. He was disappointed when Jimmy told him they could not arrest her without a warrant.

"Make up something and get it done quickly!" Paul screamed in response. "We need to take her cell phone before she alerts the other suspects."

***

Paul's warning was a little too late. Sally had already contacted Stephanie about the US Marshalls at Tameka's home.

"Are you serious?" Stephanie asked.

Sally nodded as she drove out of Tameka's community. "I'm afraid so."

"Do you know why they were there?"

"I'm not sure, but it may have something to do with the SCG scheme." Sally paused before saying, "I thought you got rid of Paul Alexander."

"I did. Why do you ask?"

"I spoke to him earlier and I just spotted him backing out of Tameka's driveway. I ducked down in my car but I think he noticed me."

"This is not good," Stephanie said as she paced back and forth in her office. "I just knew we left him for dead."

"I don't think it worked."

"Obviously!" Stephanie retorted in anger. She was mad at herself for not making sure Paul did not survive from being isolated in a deserted area for more than twenty-four hours. After calming her nerves, she asked Sally, "Do you think Tameka snitched on us?"

"It's possible. Her signature is on all the fake pensioner accounts."

"Damn it!" Stephanie screamed before becoming paranoid and vulnerable.

"Just stay calm and don't give in under pressure. We will be absolved because there is no evidence to link us to the fake pensioners."

"I don't know Sally." Stephanie looked around her office and felt so alone.

"You need to pull it together, now," Sally replied in a firm tone. "There is no time to be weak. I gotta go, but I'll be in touch."

"But wait. Do you think I should go home?"

"No, that's not a good idea. You should pretend as though you don't know anything. The less you say, the better."

"What about you?"

"Don't worry about me. I'll be fine."

"Thanks, Sally. I'll call Eddie to let him know what's going on."

Sally disconnected the call and headed home. She had been planning for this moment from the time she got involved in the embezzlement scheme. She had traded the money she received from fake pensioners and invested in bitcoins. The last time she checked, her bitcoin investment was valued at over a million dollars. The investment was not in her name, so Sally had enough money to travel around the world undetected. It also helped that the bitcoin account was not in her name.

Chapter 52

Friend or Foe

SCG Deputy Directors, Eddie and Brian, were having a good time at the local sports bar. Even though they had just met, they acted like buddies talking about every sports-game that played on several TV monitors scattered throughout the bar. The restaurant was unusually crowded because the Orioles were playing the Boston Red Sox.

While hedging bets on the game, Eddie and Brian chowed down on BLT sandwiches and drank coca cola out of sixteen-ounce Mason jars. Eddie was rooting for the Orioles and Brian was rooting for their opponent.

"How long have you known the Acting Director?" Eddie asked Brian before taking a bite out of his sandwich.

"Not too long," Brian replied without hesitation. He knew his colleague was prying. So he made sure to keep his answers and lies short and to the point.

"Have you two ever worked together?" Eddie persisted.

Brian shook his head. "No."

"Do you trust him?"

"I'm not sure," Brian said after taking a sip of soda. "Do you think he's trustworthy?"

Eddie was thrown off balance by Brian's question. He stumbled for the right response. "I...just...was under the impression that Paul Alexander hand-picked you for the job."

Brian forced a frown. "I don't know about that. I was prepared to become a Branch Chief for the Department of Defense before my supervisor informed me of this job."

"Really?"

Brian nodded. "I guess it helps that I have experience working with SCG."

"I suppose you're right." At that moment, Eddie felt assured that his new Co-Deputy and Paul were not in co-hoots. He began to view Brian as a friend, rather than a foe.

"Are you sure you don't want to get a beer?" Eddie asked as he finished off the pitcher of coke.

Brian shook his head after checking his watch. "No, we're still on the clock. We have to return to work sober." He chuckled light-heartedly.

"What's one beer?" Eddie egged on.

"One too many while we are on the clock." Brian retrieved his wallet and threw a twenty-dollar bill on the countertop. "That should be enough to cover my share."

When Brian stood up to leave, Eddie retrieved a twenty-dollar bill from his wallet and left it on the table. The waitress thanked them for the ten-dollar tip.

As they left the sports bar, Brian retrieved his cell phone from his pocket and noticed he had a missed call from Paul. He made a mental note to call the SCG Director upon returning to the office. Then he climbed in the driver's seat of his car and waited for Eddie to climb into the passenger seat.

Eddie hesitated before he entered Brian's car. He started breaking out in sweat after retrieving his cell phone from his coat pocket and scanning the text messages from Stephanie.

220

"You can drop me off at my car," Eddie said after he climbed in the passenger's seat and buckled up.

Brian frowned. "What's going on?"

"I have an urgent matter to take care of at the house. Um…my wife…it's important."

Brian turned to his new colleague with worry lines on his forehead. "Is she okay?"

"Yeah…um…she needs some help around the house." Eddie was kicking himself for not thinking of a better lie. *Damn! I'm losing it!*

"Okay," Brian slowly replied, after he figured out Eddie was lying.

"I'll sign out of work and submit a leave slip from my home office."

There was complete silence in the car during the ten-minute drive to the SCG building. Brian tried to make small talk but Eddie's non-responses did not make it palatable. He turned on the satellite radio in his car to the eighties music station and focused on the traffic.

Chapter 53

Plan B

Stephanie was locked up in her office mulling over her phone conversation with Sally Bates, the Administrative Assistant. She was scared of being implicated in the SCG scheme. She needed to talk with someone but knew her daughters were tending to the horses on their farm in Adamstown, Maryland. After reaching her oldest daughter, Becky, she explained that they needed to find a way to get rid of the SCG Director.

"Mom, what are you talking about? We left him in Pennsylvania for the buzzards. Do you remember?"

"It didn't work," Stephanie solemnly replied after chewing on her nails. "He's still alive, and he's back in Maryland."

"Damn," Becky uttered under her breath. She did not want Paul to die, but she wanted him to go away for her mother's sake.

Becky knew her mother would have a conniption if she were to discover that her daughter had something to do with Paul's survival. On the same day Paul was kidnapped, Becky had returned to Pennsylvania and left the stack of clothes, boots, a canteen of water, a pocketknife and two energy bars on the ground next to his seemingly lifeless body. She knew he was still alive and did not want to be responsible for his demise.

"We have to do something," Stephanie said in a panicky tone."

"Mom, there is nothing else for us to do."

"We don't have a choice. Getting rid of him once and for all, will ensure he doesn't become a thorn in my ass."

"But Mom, we tried…."

"Don't but me!" Stephanie shouted, then quickly lowered her voice. "Do you want to go to jail?"

"Of course not, but…."

"Just shut your face and listen to me! I need you and your sister to pack some things and leave town."

"Why?"

"Because I don't want the FBI showing up at my front door asking questions."

"For how long?"

"As long as it takes for me to kill the Director. It's obvious that I can no longer depend on you."

Becky frowned. "You can't be serious."

"I worked too hard to gain everything we own. I'll be damned if I let this City-Slicker take everything from me."

"What if…you go to jail?"

"No one is going to jail. Just leave town until I tell you it's safe to return. Use the credit cards in the top dresser drawer in my bedroom for expenses."

Becky was suddenly afraid for her mother. She knew from years of experience that she could not talk her mother out of her haphazard plans. "Where are you?" she asked after a short pause.

"At work. I'm sticking around until I get some answers from Eddie."

"Be careful, Mom. I love you."

"I love you too, Sweetie."

Stephanie disconnected the call and headed for Eddie's office. She could not understand why he did not respond to her calls or text messages.

As she strolled down the hallway, she was surprised to see her Director walking toward her. She did not know if she should pretend she did not see him and bolt in another direction. Or, if she should continue walking in his direction and appear happy to see him. When Paul's eyes connected with hers, the latter option was the only option.

"Hello, Mr. Alexander." Stephanie greeted him with a plastered smiled. "I mean, Paul. I didn't see you earlier so I assumed you were absent today."

"Hello Stephanie." Paul's fake smile matched hers. "It's good to see you. I was feeling under the weather but I feel better now. So I decided to come in and get some work done." He smirked, before admitting, "I have some unfinished business to take care of. Besides, you know that old saying, 'When the cat's away, the mice will play.'"

Stephanie threw her head back and burst out laughing like a hyaena. Her smile and laughter were fake but she played the part well. "Paul, you are so funny! What am I going to do with you?" she asked while lightly punching his shoulder.

Paul grinned. "I'm sure you will figure something out. Would love to continue chatting with you, but I have to prepare for a business meeting."

Stephanie nodded in understanding. "I don't want to hold you. But uh…um, I'm looking for Tameka. Have you seen her?"

"Why do you ask?"

"She did not report to work today, and I'm just wondering if she's okay."

"I'm sure she's fine," Paul said as he peered at his deputy's office, which was several feet away. He thought it was odd that the door was closed. "Do you know if Eddie is back from lunch?"

Stephanie shook her head. "No."

"Tell him I need to see him when he returns to work."

"Will do, boss!" Stephanie said while saluting with an airy wave of the hand.

She smiled with jubilance, but Paul was tired of playing footsie with the enemy. He was certain she was trying to glean information about Tameka.

On route to his office, Paul briefly looked back to find Stephanie staring at him with a stupid grin on her face. He couldn't stand the sight of her so he upped his speed.

Stephanie watched Paul head down the aisle toward his office until he was out of her sight. One thing she believed for sure was that Tameka did not snitch on her. Stephanie determined that had her co-worker snitched, the FBI would have arrested her by now. Besides, the FBI was more interested in solving Cyrus Hampton's murder.

Taking a deep breath and exhaling, she began to let her guard down. She returned to her office with a false sense of assurance.

Chapter 54

Sick to Death

Brian Jeffs was less than five minutes away from the job. Focusing on the traffic ahead, he continued to respect that his passenger was quiet and reserved. He glanced at Eddie and noticed he did not look well. He assumed his passenger might have had indigestion from gulping down two BLT sandwiches with a large coke. Then he guessed Eddie might be dreading going home, especially if he was telling the truth about needing to leave work to help his wife around the house.

Eddie did not pay attention to Brian, the throwback music blaring from the speakers, or the traffic on the road. He was mentally processing Stephanie's last text message: CALL ME! US MARSHALLS ARE IN FRONT OF TAMEKA'S HOME!

Suddenly light-headed, Eddie's hand flew to his chest and his heart started beating rapidly. A sharp pain penetrated his heart. "Oh...my...God," he said through faint, choppy breaths.

"What's the matter!" Brian asked, alarmed by Eddie's disposition.

"I...can't...." Eddie could not form the words for what he was trying to say. He began gasping for air as sweat bullets flooded his face.

"Hang in there. I'm taking you to the hospital."

Brian's 'pressure under fire' stance took control. He kept his left hand on the wheel while using his right hand to open his glove compartment for his safety kit. Then he quickly ruffled through the items in the small bag for aspirin.

"Thank God," he muttered under his breath, before ripping off the corner of the two-tablet packet with his teeth.

"Take these," he said as he handed the aspirin to Eddie.

"I can't…," Eddie mumbled while still gasping from air.

Brian turned to Eddie when he reached the next traffic light. "Either take them or be prepared to die from a heart attack."

The decision was a no-brainer. Eddie took the aspirin and swallowed them dry. In less than a minute, his breathing returned to normal and his heart ache lessened. He felt a little better. "Thank you," he said after taking deep breaths and exhaling.

"Don't thank me yet. You are not out of the woods," Brian added as he drove to the emergency room entrance. He parked his car, then ran into the hospital for help. Seconds later, he returned to his car with an emergency room medical technician. Brian and the technician helped Eddie climb out the car before putting him in the wheelchair.

"But I feel better," Eddie protested.

The EMT said, "You need an EKG cat scan to be sure."

"But…."

"No buts," Brian interjected. "I'll call your wife to let her know you are here."

"Thank you," Eddie said with his eyes before the EMT wheeled him through the emergency room double doors.

Brian did not have a phone number for Eddie's wife. So he returned to his car to retrieve his cell phone. He called the HR department and asked that they call Eddie's wife to let her know her husband was in the hospital. He was getting ready to call Paul but, suddenly, he heard another cell phone ringing. Brian searched around his car and found Eddie's cell phone inside the slot attached to the passenger door. He picked up the cell phone and the caller ID showed: WIFEY.

"Is this Mrs. Rosenthal?" Brian answered the ringing cell phone with caution.

"Yes, this is MaryJo. Who is this? And why are you answering my husband's phone?"

Brian explained his position at SCG. Then he informed her that Eddie was in the hospital.

MaryJo's mouth flew open in response. "Is Eddie okay?"

"I believe so. I think he would feel better if you were here with him. He's at the Inova Mount Vernon Hospital in Alexandria, Virginia."

"I know where that is. I'm on my way."

Brian disconnected the call but curiosity got the best of him. He remembered his passenger was on his phone before the heart attack. Perusing through Eddie's cell phone, Brian noticed missed calls from Stephanie. He became alarmed when he read her last text message.

"This is not good," Brian muttered under his breath. "She was trying to warn him."

After throwing Eddie's cell phone on the passenger seat, Brian hurriedly retrieved his cell phone from his suit pocket to call his Director. He grew impatient as his call went straight to

Paul's voicemail. He sent a text message instead. WE NEED TO TALK. ON MY WAY BACK TO OFFICE.

Chapter 55

Chickens Come Home to Roost

Paul was on the phone with Elizabeth 'Liz' Sanchez Varona, the President of the United States, when Brian called. He desperately wanted and needed to talk with his deputy but Liz' call took precedence. He jotted down Brian's name before resuming his conversation with the President.

The Whitehouse Senior Advisor, Jimmy Johnson, had brought Liz up to speed about the status of the SCG investigation. Though, she wanted Paul to fill her in on Tameka Collin-Brown's request for immunity in exchange for testifying about her role. "Paul, do you trust Mrs. Brown is telling the truth?"

Paul nodded. "I'm almost certain. She has everything to lose if she lies."

"Does the new deputy know what's going on?"

"Not yet. I'll let him know when he returns to the office."

"What about warrants to arrest the others?"

"You can get the ball rolling on your end. I have all the information I need to close the investigation."

"That's good, Paul. I appreciate your help on this. I could only imagine the political fallout if this matter would have been leaked to the public."

"You know me. I'm discreet."

Liz smiled. "I appreciate that. That's why I asked for your help. But I'm sorry you were tortured in the process."

Paul sniggered after recollecting the flattened tire, the fake snakes, the kidnapping, and the scavenger hunt to find his car. "I'll go through anything for you, my love."

"Uh!" Liz' cheeks flushed before she burst out in laughter. "You are such a charmer, even under the direst circumstances."

"It takes one to know one," Paul countered in a joking manner. Then he chuckled when Liz abruptly ended the call.

As soon as Paul disconnected the phone, Brian entered his office panting and nearly out of breath. "I'm so happy...to see you," he said between two deep breaths.

"Where were you?" Paul asked while trying to make sense of Brian's frantic state. "I've been trying to reach you for the past couple of hours."

"Sorry about that. Must've been a bad connection at the sports bar. Me and Eddie went there for lunch. We were returning to work but I had to take him to the hospital."

Paul leaned across his desk and stared at Brian with disbelief. "Have a seat and start from the beginning."

Brian went through the whole spiel about Eddie trying to probe his relationship with Paul. Then he told the Director that he believed Eddie had a heart attack after receiving Stephanie's text message. He paused, after asking, "Why was the Secret Service at Tameka's home? Isn't she the HR Team Leader?"

Paul nodded. "That is correct. Tameka Collins-Brown has confessed to being a part of a scheme embezzling money from fake pensioners. She's been approved for the Witness Protection Program in exchange for her cooperation. But she's not the only culprit."

"Both Eddie Rosenthal and Stephanie McPherson are involved, right?"

"Yes, but there are other accomplices."

"Really?"

"I spotted the Administrative Assistant sitting in her car not too far from Tameka Brown's home. She tried to duck but I knew it was her. Mrs. Brown told me that Sally is also involved in the scheme."

"Damn!" Brian exclaimed after sitting back in his chair and shaking his head in disbelief. "This is some gruesome shit."

Paul nodded in agreement. "Evidently, everyone involved had at least three fake accounts that receive monthly pension money. Mrs. Brown told me she believed the ploy began more than a year ago."

"That's a lot of money. What's going to happen now?

"I requested warrants be issued for Eddie Rosenthal, Stephanie McPherson, Sally Bates, and Barrett Pike."

"Do you think anyone else is involved?"

"I'm not sure. Tameka Brown has admitted to signing off on the fake pensioners but we do not have physical proof that the others were involved. The IT Team Leader has put every obstacle in place to prevent me from accessing the database. Without evidence, the others may walk."

Paul paused, before explaining, "Barret Pike placed bugs in the SCG database, which is making it virtually impossible to obtain the evidence we need. Your brother is the only one that I can think of that can hack into the system."

Brian shook his head while muttering, "Not a good idea. Can't we find someone suitable from the NSA or from the company that designed the system?"

"Oracle designed the system but it'll take too long to cut through red tape. Also contacting the NSA is out of the question. The President doesn't want too many hands in the pot - if you know what I mean."

Brian blew out air in frustration before retrieving his cell phone to call the last contact information he had for his brother. A woman answered his call on the first ring. "Hello, is Charlie available?"

"Who is this?" the woman answered in a sultry tone.

"His brother."

"Hmm…. how are you?"

"It doesn't matter. Is Charlie there?"

"Are you single?"

Brian glared at Paul, shook his head, and responded in a firm tone. "I'm going to disconnect the call if you don't put Charlie on the phone."

"What's in it for me?"

Brian was going to give her a flippant response until his brother appeared on the phone. "Hi Brian. Sorry about that. My girlfriend is tripping. You have any more money for me?"

"I want to send for you."

"Why?"

"I have a job for you."

"You do?" Charlie's eyes widened from surprise. "How much does the job pay?"

Brian covered the mouthpiece of his cell phone with his hand. He told Paul, "My brother wants to know how much he will get paid to perform the job."

"Two-thousand dollars." Paul thought that was a reasonable starting price.

Charlie was floored when his brother told him about the offer. "Make it five-thousand-dollars," he countered, "plus airfare and a hotel for me and my girlfriend."

Paul nodded in agreement after hearing Charlie's offer.

Brian asked his brother, "Can you get on a plane in the morning?"

"Yeah, but I don't have money for a cab and two plane tickets."

"I'll send an Uber to get you to the Miami International airport. A chauffeur will pick you up from the Dulles Airport when your plane lands in Virginia," Brian added after getting instructions from Paul.

"Thanks, man!" Charlie replied with excitement in his voice.

"Just…try to stay sober until you get the job done."

"You can count on me," Charlie boasted with his chest sticking out. "You won't regret this."

Brian disconnected the call and turned to Paul with worry lines across his forehead. "I'm not sure if sending for my brother is a good idea. I may not be able to get rid of him."

"Money talks, especially if he can successfully hack into the SCG database to get the evidence we need."

Paul proceeded to tell Brian what was discussed at the White House, in relation to the evidence and the fake pensioners. He paused when he heard rumblings outside his office door. He quickly stood up and rushed to open the door with Brian on his heels.

The FBI was present and in full force. They were scattered throughout the building.

"Looks like the cavalry has arrived," Brian said as he stood next to Paul and witnessed the men in black and white suits rounding up the culprits. Stephanie and Barrett were handcuffed, escorted out of the building, and thrown in the backseat of waiting sedans.

Chapter 56

Premonition

Based on Eddie's dire medical condition, he was admitted into the hospital right away. His vital signs were stable, but the doctor told him coronary heart bypass surgery was inevitable. The recent angiogram showed an eighty-percent blockage in his artery.

"We need to prep you for surgery asap," the doctor explained.

Eddie shook his head. "No, doc. I'm not sure surgery is a good idea."

His wife, MaryJo, became alarmed when she heard her husband's response. She had been sitting in a chair next to his bed since she arrived at the hospital. "Why are you fighting this?" MaryJo asked out of genuine concern. "I want you to feel better."

"It's over for me." Eddie was sad and tired. He did not want surgery, because he did not want to get well enough to possibly spend the rest of his life in jail.

The doctor looked at MaryJo before directing his attention to his patient. "If you don't get surgery right away, your chances of survival are grim."

Eddie nodded. "I know."

"I'll leave it to you two to decide what's best. In the meantime, we will continue to monitor your heart and make sure you get plenty of fluids in your IV, to relieve some pressure around your heart. Stress is not your friend, so try to relax. We will do everything in our power to save your life."

"Doctor," MaryJo called out before he turned to leave. "What will happen if my husband doesn't get surgery."

The doctor gazed at Eddie, before admitting, "We won't be able to save his life." Then he walked out of the room and closed the door behind him.

"Eddie," MaryJo said as she held his right hand and looked into his eyes. "Please reconsider surgery."

"MaryJo, I love you so much," he said in a hushed whisper. "I made some stupid decisions and I have to deal with the consequences. I don't want you or my son visiting me behind bars. Let me choose my path while I have a little dignity left."

Eddie paused to catch his breath before continuing. "I have a life insurance policy that will be enough to take care of you and put our son through the graduate program. In the meantime, remember the plan."

Tears flowed from MaryJo's eyes as her husband's words hit her hard. She could not stop crying and Eddie was too weak to console her. A day earlier, they had discussed the possibility of his arrest. He had informed her to take all the money out of their bank account and leave town.

"Where will I go?" she asked, as she sat across from him on the sofa.

"I don't know but staying here is not an option."

"What will we tell our son?"

"Tell him I want him to make good decisions in life."

"What about an attorney? Maybe an attorney can help us keep you out of jail."

Shaking his head, Eddie was doubtful of his wife's stance. "It'll be a waste of money. I approved all the fake pensioners, including the fake accounts I created for us. Then I used the money to invest in a pyramid scheme that turned out to be a scam. I was able to repay the money to all the investors." He paused to catch his breath. "My efforts to steal money from the government was a waste of time. There is no defense for my actions."

"But you told me the Director can't get in the database to verify that you signed off on those pensioners."

"I know…but this is the federal government. Where there's a will, there's a way."

"Let's just hope and pray they never find out."

"My gut tells me I'm doomed. Stephanie McPherson is a loose cannon, Tameka Collins-Brown is a scared, little mouse, and Barrett Pike has a gambling addiction that causes him to make impulsive decisions."

"What about Sally, the Administrative Assistant?" his wife asked with a glimmer of hope.

"I'm not sure about Sally. She's sharp and so far, she hasn't made any errors that I'm aware of."

"Can we trust her?"

"I think we can." Eddie turned to his wife and forced a smile. "Try not to worry."

"I can't leave you to rot in jail. Maybe you can make a deal."

"I thought about that, but everyone gave their word that we wouldn't rat on each other."

"Screw them! We have to save ourselves."

Eddie shook his head. He knew MaryJo would never understand that his word was his bond. Loyalty mattered when he was in the Navy, and still mattered at that moment.

***

Snapping back to the present, MaryJo sat back in the chair and watched the heart monitor. Eddie's blood pressure seemed to decrease with each passing minute. She wanted to be strong for him, especially after the doctor told her he cannot endure added stress at this critical time.

All of a sudden, she freaked out when the FBI agents burst into the room and handcuffed Eddie to the hospital bed. Another FBI agent read him his rights while MaryJo stood up screaming hysterically. "You can't do this!" she insisted, trying to remove one of the handcuffs from her husband's wrist. "My husband can't deal with this right now. He has a heart problem! Can't you see that?" she asked, pointing to the IV and heart monitor machine.

The FBI agent pulled MaryJo away from Eddie and sat her in the chair next to the hospital bed. "Ma'am, we need you to calm down or you will be escorted out of the hospital."

"Do you have to do this now?" MaryJo sobbed uncontrollably.

"Ma'am, your husband is a suspect in a fraud scheme."

"Please calm down," Eddie pleaded in a bare whisper. "You know what you need to do."

"But I can't leave you like this."

"I don't want you to stay here, to watch me die. Please go."

Nimbly, MaryJo stood up and kissed Eddie on the cheek. "I love you. I will always love you." She grabbed her pursed and walked out of the hospital room.

As soon as she drove away from the hospital, Eddie went into cardiac arrest. His heart machine started beeping nonstop before it flatlined. The doctors rushed into the room with a defibrillator to restore his heartbeat. Their efforts proved futile. Eddie passed away while the FBI agents stood outside his hospital room.

Chapter 57

Anonymous Tipster

The FBI was still working to solve Cyrus Hampton's murder when they spoke with his wife. She had been ruled out as a suspect after they verified that she was in Florida taking care of her mother when her husband was murdered.

The FBI did not have any leads until they received an anonymous tip that Sally Bates may have something to do with how Cyrus was murdered. The mysterious person indicated that Sally may have killed her husband with poisoned berries, and Cyrus was probably killed in the same manner. The tipster explained that Sally's husband was a Scientist with the Center for Disease Control, and he was exploring the benefits of the exotic berries.

The FBI checked out the tipster's allegation and was able to verify that Sally's husband worked with the berries at the CDC. Her husband was cremated. So they could not run a toxicology test to verify that he was poisoned.

The FBI was determined to find answers. They arrived at Sally's home in full force, but she was nowhere in sight. Though, the warrant gave them permission to search her home.

After bursting through the locks on the front door, the FBI discovered no one was home. The house was fully furnished and the utilities were still active. A thorough search in the bedroom revealed that some of Sally clothes in her dressers and closet were missing.

The agents looked in the freezer and became alarmed at the sight of frozen berries wrapped in Styrofoam. The FBI Chemist verified that the exotic berries are the same berries that poisoned Cyrus Hampton.

After consulting with the Food and Drug Administration, the FBI Chemist learned that the berries were from a remote area in South America. The chemist also discovered that the berries are white and poisonous in the winter, but they are safe to eat when they turn red in the summer months. He understood that the berries stayed white during the summer by storing them in a freezer. The Chemist gathered that the frozen poisoned berries were mixed with red food quality dye and strawberries in the shake that Cyrus Hampton drank.

Based on the evidence, the FBI was certain Sally Bates was a primary suspect in Cyrus' murder.

Chapter 58

Lights, Camera, Action!

Paul called a quick staff meeting shortly after the FBI arrested and escorted Stephanie and Barrett out of the building. He was certain that everyone witnessed the commotion, so he called the meeting to put everyone at ease. He requested that Brian Jeffs stand next to him at the podium. Then he waited until the last person entered the conference room before thanking everyone for their attendance under short notice.

"Good afternoon," Paul began. "Earlier, the FBI arrested two of our staff members for allegedly committing fraud here at the Select Committee for General Services. I'm sure you have questions but I cannot reveal any information until the investigation is complete. However, we encourage the entire staff to report any fraud and abuse that occurs at our Agency or any other government entity.

SCG handles sensitive data, and our clients trust that we do everything necessary to ensure that their identity and data is protected. As your Acting Director, I am committed to making sure SCG continues to provide efficient and invaluable service to our clients."

One staff member raised her hand and stood up, before asking, "Is anyone else going to be arrested?"

"The investigation is ongoing."

Another staff member stood up and stated, "I heard they arrested Eddie Rosenthal. Is that true?"

"I'm not at liberty to reveal any information about the investigation at this time. However, your new Deputy Director, Brian Jeffs, will take over Eddie Rosenthal's duties for now. Brian has not had the opportunity to introduce himself to everyone. But he will be stopping by your desk to personally speak to each of you throughout the week."

"What about Tameka Collins-Brown?" another staffer yelled out. "I don't see her here. Does that mean she's been arrested?"

"I can't answer your question. But I can assure you that the FBI is only interested in those that allegedly committed fraud."

"Is the investigation still active?" another staff member asked.

Paul was prepared to respond until some staff members huddled and started talking amongst themselves. "Please…simmer down," he said while extending his arm with the palm of his hand faced down. "We will answer all of your questions when the time is right."

Scanning the room, Paul felt uneasiness in the air. He knew the employees were on edge over the arrests. Nodding, he knew there was nothing more he could have said to lessen their concerns. He concluded the meeting by saying, "This Agency will not falter in its mission."

Brian followed the Director out of the conference room leaving the SCG staff staring into space. "Damn, that was intense," he said as soon as they entered Paul's office.

Paul nodded. "I know. Can you imagine what it was like on my first day?"

"I can only imagine. But you're good under pressure."

Paul chuckled. "Never let them see you sweat. As former Navy men, we learned to live by the creed. Duty, Honor…"

"…and Country," they said in unison.

"Paul, I'll catch up with you later. I'm going to start making the rounds to introduce myself."

"That's a great idea. But don't forget the package we have to retrieve from the airport in the morning."

"Don't remind me." Brian's smile quickly turned upside down.

"I wouldn't ask if it wasn't important."

Brian turned to leave but Paul made a gesture for him to stay after his cell phone rang. "Hold up for a second. The President is on the line. Have a seat and close the door."

"Liz," Paul said, after he put the call on speaker, "you must've been reading my mind. I was getting ready to call you."

"Hello Paul. I wanted to touch base before news went out on the rumor mill."

"What's going on?"

"The FBI told me Eddie Rosenthal just died from a heart attack. He was in the hospital but refused coronary surgery."

"Damn," Brian uttered under his breath.

"That's really unfortunate," Paul replied. "Does his wife know?"

Liz nodded. "Yes, she was there by his bedside when he told her to leave. I was told Eddie did not want her to watch him die."

Paul sighed. "I just wish he would've told the truth."

"Well, the news doesn't get any better. I just learned that Stephanie McPherson and Barrett Pike will be able to post bail in the morning. Considering what you've been through, I can send Secret Service to protect you until the trial is over."

"That's not necessary. I'll be fine. What about Sally Bates?"

"We couldn't find her. It seems she's disappeared in thin air. But don't worry. We will find her, especially since we want to question her about her role in Cyrus Hampton's murder."

"Are you serious?"

"I'm afraid so. We received an anonymous tip that Sally Bates' deceased husband was a Scientist for the Center for Disease Control. He happened to be working with the exotic berries that killed Cyrus Hampton. The tipster also stated they believe that was how Sally killed her husband."

Paul frowned. "I understand the motive for killing Cyrus Hampton. But what would be the motive for killing her husband?"

"We're not sure, which is why we desperately need to find and bring her in for questioning."

Paul took a deep breath and exhaled. "This is a lot to absorb."

"But the good news is that we were able to get Tameka Collins-Brown settled in her new home, in a secret location. We were also able to convince her mother to enter the Witness Protection program with her daughter. Initially, she resisted the offer but gave in after we convinced her that this will only be a temporary arrangement, and she'll be able to return to her familiar surroundings after the investigation is over." Liz paused, before asking, "Do you think anyone else is involved in the SCG scheme?"

"I think we have the major culprits," Paul said with confidence. "We will learn more once we are able to access the SCG database and put a stop payment on the fake pensioner accounts."

"Do you know when that will happen?"

Paul glanced at Brian and smirked. "Liz, I have someone coming from out of town in the morning. I believe he will be able to access the SCG database and stop the payments for the fake pensioners with no problem."

"I don't want to hear anymore," she quickly interjected after fearing furtherance of the conversation was going to reveal something unethical or illegal. "I'm sure you've already discussed this matter with my Senior Advisor. Just let me know the end results."

"I understand. I'll touch base with you tomorrow." Paul snickered after Liz disconnected the call.

Brian frowned after noticing the way Liz abruptly ended the call. "Is that the norm?"

Paul nodded. "That's the norm."

Chapter 59

Out on Bond

Stephanie felt uneasy about her predicament. Before the FBI arrested her, she hired the best attorney her embezzled money could buy. He was the best in the tri-State area. She had also convinced him to represent the IT Team Leader, since she was privy to Barrett's financial situation.

The attorney was certain to get an arraignment and bail hearing for Stephanie and Barrett as soon as they were taken into custody. The next day, their bail was set at fifty-thousand dollars. The bail was low because the government could not assess a monetary value of the embezzled money.

Stephanie was relieved, her co-worker, Barrett, did not take a plea deal in exchange for giving the Director access to the SCG database system. Stephanie figured Barrett had more to lose than she did. Everyone at the job knew he owed loan sharks a large sum of money and repaying them with money from fake pensioner accounts helped keep them at bay.

"What are we going to do now?" Barrett asked after they walked out of the hearing.

"My attorney told me they don't have enough evidence to make the charges stick. Can you assure me that no one can access the SCG database?"

"I'm the best there is. I created a fail-switch that will shut down the whole system and erase all the pensioners if anyone tried to access the system."

"How does that work?"

"It's complicated but I got us covered."

"Does it mean the checks will stop?"

"Yes. The fail-switch will activate as soon as someone access the database. An alert will appear on the system that states: ALL PENSIONERS WILL BE DELETED FROM SYSTEM."

Stephanie nodded her approval. "You are clever."

"Only the best."

"I have business to handle. But I need you to stay low for a while."

"What are you going to do?"

"Get rid of the missing link, and don't ask any questions."

"Gotcha!"

When Barrett walked out of the courthouse, Stephanie retrieved her cell phone from her purse and called her eldest daughter. She was relieved Becky answered her call on the first ring. "Are you and your sister okay?"

"We are fine. How are you?"

"Just got out of a stinking cell. Other than that, I'm okay. Where are you girls?"

"In a hotel in downtown Baltimore."

"You idiot!" Stephanie screamed to the top of her lungs. "I told you to get out of town."

"We didn't want to be too far from you, in case you were released on bond."

Stephanie calmed down after realizing her daughter made the right decision. "Swing by the courthouse to get me, so we can go home."

"Do you think that's a good idea?"

"Why are you questioning my decisions?"

"I just thought…."

"Well don't think. I'll do the thinking for both of us. Besides, we have some unfinished business to take care of."

Becky bit her bottom lip after willing herself not to ask any more questions. "You know what's best, Mom."

"Now that's what I like to hear."

Chapter 60

One-Eighty

Charlie and his girlfriend arrived at the Dulles airport as scheduled. Both wreaked of alcohol and looked exhausted after the three-hour flight. They walked out the arrival exit and were greeted by a Secret Service Agent.

"Charlie Jeffs?" the agent asked to be sure.

"That's me, Buddy. And this is my girl."

"Nice to meet both of you. Where are your bags?" the agent asked, after looking at their empty hands.

Charlie's girlfriend said, "We don't have any."

"Okay, please follow me. You are scheduled to meet with your brother and Paul Alexander, the Director of the Select Committee for General Services," the agent said as he led them to the car. "But first, I will take you to the hotel to freshen up."

"Sounds good, but we're hungry," Charlie said after following his girlfriend in the backseat of the black sedan." Can you swing by McDonalds to get us something to eat?"

"Yeah, I'm hungry," Charlie's girlfriend chimed in.

The agent looked at his watch. "We are pressed for time. I was instructed to take you to the hotel. But I'll make sure food is available to you by the time we arrive."

Charlie nodded. "Sounds like a plan."

The agent forced a smile but he was having a hard time enduring their awful, smelly, body odor. He tried to be discreet by cracking the windows but the whistling sound from the window was more annoying than the smell. He sped up and arrived at the hotel in twenty minutes, which typically took thirty minutes from the airport.

"We're here," the agent said before he quickly parked in front of the hotel and climbed out of the car. He was getting ready to open the back door for Charlie and his girlfriend, but they were already outside the car taking in the elegant surroundings.

"This is nice," Charlie said after spotting the formally dressed bell hopper. "So this is what first-class feels like."

"Sir," the agent said, "the hotel has a boutique where you can obtain clothing and anything else you need to freshen up."

"I don't have any money."

"It's okay. It'll be a government expense. Feel free to pick up everything you need."

The agent entered the boutique first to explain to the clerk he would be using a government credit card to pay for Charlie and his girlfriend's purchases. He further explained that there was no set limit."

The clerk nodded in understanding. Over the next hour, he assisted Charlie and his girlfriend with picking out clothing, underwear, shoes, and the gambit. Then the agent gave them their room key and told them he had placed their food order which would be delivered to the room. Next, he directed his attention to Charlie, and said, "I will meet you downstairs in an hour."

"That's not enough time for me to take a shower and eat."

"I suggest you take a shower and grab a snack. You have a job to do. I was tasked with making sure you report to work on time."

"What about me?" the girlfriend inquired.

"You can stay at the hotel and enjoy the amenities."

She beamed with delight. "I like that. You think I can get a spa treatment?" she asked the agent.

"Sure, bill everything you need to the room."

Charlie asked, "When do I get the money?"

"When the job is completed. But time is of the essence."

"I'll go get ready."

An hour later, Charlie came downstairs to meet up with the agent. He was clean-shaven, dressed in jeans and a polo shirt, and smelled like a fresh bar of soap.

The agent nodded his approval of Charlie's appearance. It only took a short time for him to get on to the main highway, which was a quick route to the SCG building.

Chapter 61

Cliffhanger

When Barrett left the courthouse, he did not know he was being followed. Two tall, burly looking men were in a car following his every move. They continued to follow Barrett when he climbed in an Uber to go to the casino at the MGM National Mall in Oxon Hill, Maryland.

Barrett was desperate. He had agreed to pay his loan sharks over one-hundred-thousand dollars, three days earlier. That deadline had his nerves doing flips in his stomach. He had over five-hundred dollars in his pocket. In his head, he more than quadrupled the money ten times playing Blackjack. Barrett believed that was just enough to keep the loan sharks at bay.

Shaking his head, Barrett had a feeling his life was doomed. He did know who to be more fearful of, the FBI or the loan sharks. He got involved with the SCG scheme after realizing irregularities in the SCG database. The false pension accounts did not go through the proper protocol. He brought the issue to Eddie's attention, who bribed him in exchange for his silence. Ultimately, money from the fake pensioners only worsened his gambling habit and increased his debt to the loan sharks.

Barret closed his eyes wishing for an escape plan. Short on funds, his plans were short-lived. He decided that if he won big at the MGM casino, he would leave the U.S. and start over.

The Uber driver noticed the car behind him. He thought it was strange that the car was tailing him for over fifteen minutes. Whenever he slowed down, the car behind him slowed down. When he sped up and changed lanes, the car behind him did the same. The driver eyed Barrett in the rearview mirror, before asking, "Do you know who's following us?"

Barrett frowned. "How should I know?"

"The Lincoln Town car behind us has been following me since I left the courthouse."

"Are you sure?" Barrett asked as he turned around to get a good view of the car. His heartbeat seemed to speed up when he noticed the driver and passenger were two of the goons that work for the loan sharks.

"Damn!" Barrett exclaimed, getting antsy in his seat. "Speed up!" he frantically yelled at the driver.

"What are you talking about? I'm not exceeding the speed limit to get a ticket for you."

The car sped up and rode alongside of the Uber car. Both goons got a good look at Barrett who was curled up in the backseat. "Pull over!" the goon in the passenger seat yelled from his window.

"What is wrong with that guy?" the Uber driver asked Barrett who buried his face with his arms. "Do you know him?"

"Just drive faster!" Barrett grumbled.

"What have you gotten me into? I'm not going to ruin this car to save your life." The Uber driver drove onto the side lane and parked the car. "Get out," he told Barrett.

"They will kill me."

"I don't give a damn. I'm not risking my life for yours. I know goons when I see them. You got yourself into something your ass can't handle."

The driver of the Town car drove up behind the Uber car. Then the goon from the passenger side climbed out and ran to the rear passenger side of the Uber car. "Unlock the door," he yelled to Barrett.

When Barrett refused to unlock the door, the Uber driver happily obliged his request. "I didn't see nothing," he told the goon, who dragged Barrett out of the car like a rag doll.

The Uber driver waited until his passenger was out his car before he drove away. He stayed true to his word – he did not report the incident to the police.

Barrett was putting up an unbeatable fight with the goon as he was pushed toward the Town car and told to get in the backseat. He whimpered after climbing in the car. He knew what was next. Then he looked down at his fingers and cried like a baby.

After driving several miles to West Virginia, the goons pulled Barrett out of the car and dragged him to a cliff that was surrounded by mountains. The scenery was breathtaking. The cliff was several yards deep and the bottom contained mounds of large boulder rocks.

"Wait! Wait!" Barrett pleaded for dear life. "Um, who are you?"

"Call me Bill," the goon on the right side of Barrett replied.

"And call me Bob, the other goon on the left side of Barrett added.

"It's nice to meet you Barrett," Bill said while holding Barrett upright while his feet drag the ground. "It's okay to use your first name, isn't it Barrett."

"Sure, anything you want," Barrett replied with fear in his voice.

"I can give you some money, but I'm a little short right now. You guys are scary."

The goons burst out laughing.

"It's in our job description to be scary," Bill said while holding a tight grip on Barrett's right shoulder and arm. "Bob and I have family, wifey and kids to support. We have to deliver for the Big man to justify our salaries."

"Yeah," Bob chimed in with a booming voice. "If you are a little short on funds, we should take a little walk to the edge to discuss this matter."

"What are you going to do?" Barrett asked trying to stay away from the cliff.

"You're going to commit suicide," Bob firmly replied.

"No! No! No! Don't do this! I have money," Barrett said as he retrieved five crisp one-hundred-dollar bills from his pocket and showed it to them.

One of the goons took the money and laughed. "We can make this hard or we can make it easy. Pick one," he told Barrett with a wicked grin on his face.

"Uh…uh…what are you saying? I mean, what are the conditions? I don't understand."

"Hard or easy," the goon repeated with a serious demeanor.

"Easy, I think."

"Good choice."

Barrett did not see the other goon come up from behind him and push him over the cliff. He rolled down the cliff bouncing against several boulders before his body seemed to break in two.

The goons gave each other a high-five before taking a picture for proof of Barrett's demise.

Chapter 62

Jackpot

Brian and Paul were waiting in front of the SCG building for Charlie's arrival. Both were pleasantly surprised when he climbed out of the sedan, looking sharp.

Charlie smiled when he spotted his brother. He walked over and gave him a warm hug. "It's good to see you, Brian."

"Same here," Brian said with pride in his voice. Then he turned to Paul and made the introductions.

"I heard so much about you," Paul said while shaking Charlie's hand.

"I hope it was all good."

"It was," Paul lied to appease Charlie. "Let's go to my office to discuss our dilemma.

Over the next thirty minutes, Paul told Charlie what he learned about the SCG database and his troubles with trying to access it. He also explained the purpose of needing to access the data. "I could be wrong, but I believe bugs are in the system."

"Bugs?" Charlie asked.

"Yeah, check this out." Paul turned on his office computer and positioned it catty-corner so Brian and Charlie could see what he was doing. When he put in his credentials to enter the SCG database, a prompt appeared showing he received an error message. "If I try to enter my credentials again," Paul explained, "the system locks out on me."

"That's a fail-switch," Charlie stated with confidence.

"Come again?"

Charlie explained, "That's a program that administrators use to prevent un-authorized entry."

"How would you remove a fail-switch?"

"It's not that easy. I have to write procedures that bypass the fail-switch first, in order to remove it from the database."

"How soon can you do that?"

"I need a couple of hours and a sandwich."

"That fast?"

"Yeah," Charlie said with a nod. "I need to look at how the system is wired. If I try to remove the fail-switch without making adjustments to the mainframe, the whole system will crash and all data will disappear. Do you have a computer operation room?"

"It's downstairs. Let's go."

Paul escorted Charlie and Brian to the computer room on the first floor of the building. He told the two IT technicians that were present to leave the room for a couple of hours. After they left, he turned to Charlie and asked, "Do you know what you're looking for?"

"Yes," Charlie said as he walked over to the mainframe to assess the wiring. Then he looked at the computer monitor connected to the mainframe. He sat in front of the monitor and pressed CTRL/*123 to bypass the homepage. Suddenly, the stored procedures and hard coding for the entire SCG database appeared.

Paul asked, "What does all that coding mean?"

Charlie laughed. "Only an IT genius knows how to read coding. But it's going to take some time to figure this out."

"I'll order your sandwich," Brian said. "Do you have a preference?"

"I'm not picky. Anything will do."

Over the next hour and a half, Paul and Brian sat in silence while Charlie dissected and rewrote the coding. He also manipulated the computer wiring before rebooting the system.

"I'm ready," Charlie finally said. "It was a lot easier than I thought it would be. You were right about the bugs though. Someone purposely blocked you from accessing the database."

"I knew it. Now what?"

Charlie stood up, and said, "Let's go back to your office so you can log on to your desktop."

Upon returning to the office, Paul sat his desk while Brian and Charlie sat across from him. He turned to Charlie, and asked, "Will I get locked out if I try to enter my PIN number again?"

"Not this time."

Reluctantly, Paul entered his credentials to access the database. He was surprised when he did not get a prompt. Instead, he was able to access all the data he needed to determine who created the fake pensioners. "This is good," he said, as he turned to Charlie. "But I need one more favor."

"What is it?"

"I need you to reverse some accounts that were previously established."

"Are you sure? If I do that, those accounts will remain in the database but payment associated with those accounts will stop."

"That's exactly what I want."

"Okay, I need to return to the computer room to write some coding."

"No problem. You can go on downstairs, and I'll meet up with you later. I need to do some research on some of the accounts."

After Charlie left to go to the computer room, Paul remained glued to the computer while his deputy remained in his presence. He focused his research on the fake accounts that have already been verified by the CIA Officer.

After noticing how Paul's eyes widened, Brian asked, "Did you discover who created the fake accounts?"

"Yeah, the database confirms that Stephanie McPherson is the Senior Writer for the fake accounts that we are aware of. Looks like Eddie Rosenthal and Tameka Collins-Brown signed off on the accounts. I'm printing data for the accounts Stephanie created for the past two years. It's going to take some time to decipher the fake cases but it's necessary to stop the monthly pensions."

"What can I do to help?"

"The database shows Stephanie created over one-hundred cases." Paul jotted down the name and phone number of the CIA Officer that was able to verify the legitimacy of new identities for five individuals.

"Call the CIA Officer to see if he can lend his support?" he said as he handed Brian the note. "Tell him that I will forward the cases to him in an hour or so."

"I'm on it."

Chapter 63

Without a Trace

Prior to poisoning Cyrus Hamilton, Sally had been following him for quite some time. She had stolen his house key off his keychain a week before she murdered him. Then she snuck into his home with the poisoned shake in an ice bucket and waited in a back bedroom for him to arrive home. She figured he would go to the kitchen first, and she was right. She also presumed that adding the sticky note to the shake would compel him to drink it with no reservations.

She had eased out of the bedroom and into the hallway to watch Cyrus drink the poisoned shake. Then she watched him from afar as he fell to the floor, crawled out of his front door and onto the walkway path in front of his home.

A little part of her felt guilty for her actions, but the other part of her felt relief. She was certain Cyrus would not survive his fate. His eventual death ensured she and her comrades would continue benefiting from the fake pensioners.

As she drove away from the scene of the crime, Sally thought about her husband. Like Cyrus, he started questioning the extra money that came into their home. He had even threatened to report her after he found out she and her colleagues were embezzling money from SCG. Sally knew that could not happen. They had a big argument before she killed him. She believed his death was inevitable.

Now Sally was left to fend for herself after killing her husband and her lover. She had illegally obtained a passport from Tameka's desk, a week before Cyrus Hampton was murdered. The passport was among many, various evidentiary documents issued after SCG established a new identity for their clients. Typically, one original document was sent to the customer and a duplicate document was sent to the Director for review. The latter was subsequently released to the respective government Agency for their records.

The SCG was very careful with handling evidentiary documents and took proper measures to ensure the documents were correctly disbursed. However, in rare instances, the SCG staff would start from scratch by creating new identities if a document was misplaced or missing.

Sally knew one day the stolen passport would come in handy. She was able to fly to Canada before taking another plane to Russia under the radar. Her new features to conceal her true identity also helped. She had changed her hair color from blonde to brunette, cut off her long hair for a pixie haircut, and traded in her fancy blouses and maxi skirts for jeans and turtleneck sweaters.

Upon arriving in Russia, she checked into a hotel in St. Petersburg. Sally chose her new country because it was large in scope. It was also easy to escape captivity in remote areas. Lastly, Sally believed that it helped that Russia and the United States did not have an extradition agreement.

Chapter 64

Pay Day

Charlie worked diligently to reverse and put a stop payment on the fake accounts. His actions sent an automatic alert to the Treasury department to start the reclamation process. Within minutes, the banks were notified to return embezzled money direct deposited from the very beginning.

In the end, Treasury had recovered some of the retirement money that remained in bank accounts established by Eddie Rosenthal and Stephanie McPherson. However, accounts established by Tameka Collins-Brown and Sally Bates were closed, and Barrett Pike had a negative balance in his account. The bank would send letters to the addresses on record to try to recover the balance. Though, this action would prove futile since the accounts were not in their names.

When Charlie finished the job, Paul handed him a check for five-thousand dollars. Charlie's eyes widened at what he deemed an error. "It's not a mistake," Paul confirmed. "We reward good work."

"I appreciate that."

Brian beamed like a proud big brother before turning his attention to Paul. "If you don't mind, I'd like to speak with Charlie alone."

"Sure." Paul turned to Charlie and smiled. "It was nice meeting you. Hope to see you again, soon."

Charlie smiled in response.

"I'm proud of you Charlie," Brian sincerely admitted. "The Secret Service agent told me about your appearance when you arrived at the airport."

"Yeah," Charlie admitted as he turned around and posed to show off his new digs. "But look at me now."

"That's not what I mean. You were intoxicated when you got off that plane. Have you considered going into rehab?"

"Yeah, but I'm not ready.

"When you're ready, I will pay for rehab, and make sure you have a job and a place to live."

"You'll do that for me?"

"Let's just say I know very important people that can change your life."

"I appreciate that, but I need to get back to the hotel right now. Me and my girl are going to celebrate tonight."

"Please stay in touch," Brian said, before his brother climbed into the backseat of the waiting sedan.

"Most definitely!"

After seeing his brother off, Brian returned to Paul's office and sat at his desk. He noticed his friend was still on the computer typing away. "I hate to bother you, but are you almost done here?"

"Almost." Paul looked at the computer monitor, before turning to his friend to ask, "What do you have planned this evening?"

"I'm going to take Maria out to dinner. Then I'm going to the Baltimore Orioles baseball game. Do you want to come?"

"And be a third wheel?" Paul chuckled. "I don't think so."

"Maria doesn't like baseball. She agreed to meet me for dinner at the harbor. I'm going to the game alone after dinner."

"Well if that's the case, I would love to go to the Oriole Park at Camden Yards. The game will temporarily take my mind off everything that's going on here at the agency."

"I'm glad you said that." Brian retrieved baseball tickets from his pocket. "I wouldn't want the extra ticket to go to waste." He handed one of the tickets to Paul.

"Are you serious?" Paul asked after noticing the seat location on the tickets. "These are front row seats in front of the Pitcher's mound."

"Yep. My former colleague lost a bet. Consider it an early birthday present."

Paul stood up and shook Brian's hand. "Thanks, man."

"No problem. I'll see you at the stadium. The game starts at eight pm."

"I'll be there!"

Chapter 65

Double Whammy!

Watching the first five innings of the Baltimore Orioles vs. Boston Red Sox had Paul and Brian on edge. The pitchers for both teams had no hitters and the score remained zero to zero. In the sixth round, the Orioles were in the lead. The Boston Red Sox came back for an inning but could not hold on. The Orioles beat the Red Sox by one run. The final score was enough for Brian and Paul to celebrate their victory.

They were celebrating the good luck of Orioles or poor playing by Boston on the walk back to the cars. When suddenly, a woman approached them and pulled a pack of cigarettes out of her purse. She was wearing dark tinted sunglasses and a cap that covered her hair. Paul and Brian tried to step around her, but she moved in front of them. Red lipstick that adorned the woman's voluptuous lips stood out.

Suddenly, Paul had a flashback to the day he was kidnapped in Ellicott City, Maryland. He pushed Brian out of the way and yelled, "Run!"

Both ran opposite sides of the woman. They fumbled when they heard two gunshots behind them. Brian continued running but Paul yelped from pain in his left shoulder. He kept pounding the pavement even though he assumed he was shot.

Paul and Brian met up in the parking lot, across the street from the Orioles stadium. They had managed to put some distance between themselves and the woman.

Paul looked back to see a crowd gather but decided that it would be prudent to get out of there.

"You can't drive," Brian explained as they arrived at his car. "You've been shot."

Paul assessed the sleeve of his Oriole's jacket and noticed the small hole. A cursory examination did not reveal any blood. He removed his jacket and noticed that the bullet grazed his shoulder. Taking a deep breath and exhaling, Paul was relieved the bullet did not penetrate into his skin.

Brian shook his head in awe. "You are one lucky bastard."

"I know."

"Let's get out of here, before your luck runs out. You can ride with me."

Paul shook his head. "I drove here."

"It's obvious that someone is after you. I'm almost certain they know what you're driving. At this rate, we have to be cautious and think that things are worse."

"What could be worse than getting shot at?"

"Having your body shredded into a million pieces from a car bomb explosion."

"You're right, I'll ride with you." Paul hurriedly strutted to the passenger side of Brian's car and climbed in.

"It's time to call in the cavalry," Brian said, as he turned to Paul. "Your life is in danger. I'll take you to my place for the time being."

When Paul buckled his seatbelt, he retrieved his cell phone from his pocket and called the White House. The President answered his call on the first ring.

"Paul, are you okay?"

"Not quite," he said before explaining how he was shot at earlier.

"Oh my God. Are you sure you're okay?"

"Yeah, but my jacket took a hit." Paul chuckled, before explaining, "I think I'm going to take you up on that offer for protection until this case is over."

"You got it. I'll send a couple of agents to your home. They should be there in thirty minutes or so. Anything else you need?"

"Not that I can think of."

When Liz disconnected the call, Paul reclined on the head rest in the passenger seat and closed his eyes. He flashed back on everything that occurred to him since he took the assignment with SCG. He had a flat tire on day one. Then someone scared him nearly to death with a snake-sounding moth around his house. Lastly, he was kidnapped and left to die in rural Pennsylvania.

Shaking his head, he could not get over the fact that he had to go on a scavenger hunt to find his car in the State Park. But getting shot in a crowded baseball stadium led him to believe that the perpetrator would stop at no cost to make sure he was dead.

Chapter 66

Mommie Dearest

Shortly after Stephanie bailed out of jail, her daughter, Becky told her that the debit card did not work and she and her sister had been using the credit card to get by. "I tried using it at two different ATM machines but the card reader showed, 'INSUFFIENT FUNDS.'"

"There should be at least ten thousand dollars in that account," Stephanie replied with certainty. She knew the monthly pensions were deposited on the third of every month.

"I'm not sure why it didn't work."

"Give me that debit card, idiot! You probably entered the wrong PIN number. Pull over to the next ATM!"

Becky sighed as she got off at the next exit on I-295. She was tired of her mother's verbal abuse. Remaining mum was her only solace as she parked her car in front of the bank.

Stephanie climbed out the car and walked up to the ATM to withdraw money. She was dumbfounded when her bank balance showed zero dollars. She stormed into the bank screaming like a mad woman. "Someone stole my money!"

The teller was taken aback by Stephanie's hysteria. "Ma'am, you need to calm down. As soon as you provide your ID, we can get to the bottom of what happened."

Stephanie went into her purse to retrieve her ID. Then it dawned on her that the account she was trying to access was in the fake pensioner's name. She stalled, trying to think of a solution to her dilemma.

The teller noticed Stephanie was hesitant. "Ma'am, I can't help you without proper ID."

"Just tell me what happened to the account," Stephanie pleaded.

"I can't help you if you don't have proper ID. But maybe you can access the account online to get the answers you need."

"Mom," Becky said as she lightly reached for her mother's arm, "let's get out of here."

"Don't touch me!" Stephanie yanked her arm away from her daughter. Then she retrieved her cell phone from her purse to access the online bank account data. Her body went limp when she noticed that the funds were frozen.

"Mom, what's wrong?" Becky grew concerned about her mother's slumped posture. "Are you okay?"

Stephanie remained silent for a few seconds before she realized what probably happened. "That bastard! He won't get away with this. I'm going to kill him!"

"Mom, what are you talking about?"

"That damn Paul Alexander," Stephanie spouted through gritted teeth, "that's who I'm talking about. He tried to screw the wrong person."

Incensed, Stephanie turned into a madwoman. She wanted to exact revenge with every fiber of her being.

***

When Stephanie planned to get even with Paul, she decided to use her daughter as a pawn. She had followed him to the baseball game and watched his every move. Her patience was tested as she waited for the game to end. Stephanie was not aware that a typical Major League baseball game lasted for more than three hours.

After Paul stood up to leave, she prodded her daughter, Becky, to approach him in her sexy getup.

"Now or never," Stephanie said to herself, as she retrieved the gun and shot in his direction. She did not count on Brian Jeffs being there and pushing him out of her view. She almost panicked when her daughter fell down, presumably from the first bullet. But Stephanie could not let that deter her from accomplishing her objective.

Chasing Paul through the crowded stadium, she shot at him again. She was certain she did not miss her target after she heard him yelp from pain. Though, she did not have the luxury of standing around to watch him die. People were watching her and she had to get out of there. For a split second, she wanted to go see about Becky. The security guards headed in her direction thwarted her plan.

Stephanie was able to lose the security guards by blending in with the crowd. She had managed to get away from the Oriole's stadium without being detected. On the run from the law, Stephanie was driving at the speed of lightning and headed northbound to Canada. Her goal was to cross the border and lay low until she figured out what to do next.

Suddenly, Stephanie broke down crying after it dawned on her that she may have killed her daughter. She felt awful leaving Becky on the ground bleeding from the gunshot wound. She was hysterical as she banged her fists on the steering wheel, yelling and screaming, "God, why! Not my child! What have I done!!"

Her watershed tears blinded her vision. When she dried her eyes with the back of her hands, her car crashed into the bumper of the car in front of her. The air bags inflated and saved her head from crashing through the windshield. But her body became mangled when an eighteen-wheeler slammed into the back of her car. The impact was so severe, Stephanie's car was sandwiched between the car in front of her and the truck. She was pronounced dead on arrival by the EMTs.

Chapter 67

Glimmer of Hope

Unfortunately, Becky became the victim of her mother's rage. She was in the hospital recovering from surgery. The gunshot wound was not life-threatening, but it severely injured her leg.

The doctor performed surgery to remove the bullet and repair damage to bones, tendons, ligaments, and major blood vessels in her left leg. Then she was fitted with a brace to allow the tissues to heal after the doctor applied staples to close the wound.

Heavily medicated from pain meds, Becky opened her eyes and was surprised to see FBI agents near her bedside. "What's going on?" she asked one of the agents.

"We need to ask you questions about your mother," the FBI replied, after approaching her bed.

"Where is she?"

"She didn't make it."

"Wh...what do you mean? She didn't make what?"

"We're sorry to report that your mother was in a car accident." The agent paused, before adding, "She didn't survive the impact."

Distraught by this news, tears began pouring down her face. She was in shock but she was also numb.

"Ms. McPherson, can you tell us if you knew your mother was embezzling money from the Select Committee from General Services?"

"I don't know what you're talking about," Becky said after drying her eyes and blowing her nose with the tissue provided by the FBI agent. "I…uh…I'm tired. I need to rest."

"We understand." The agent retrieved a business card from his wallet and put it on the stand next to her bed. "Please call us if you remember anything. In particular, we need to ask you questions about the transmitters that were affixed outside the SCG Director's home."

After the agents left the room, Becky closed her eyes and felt the enormity of learning of her mother's death. For her entire life, her mother had always dictated her every move. She was not sure how she felt about her newfound freedom.

Suddenly, she felt someone's presence in her room. It was her father. Frowning, she asked, "Why are you here? You abandoned us."

"I didn't abandon you," he admitted with sincere eyes. " I had to leave your mother. She had problems that I couldn't fix."

"Why are you here?"

"Your sister told me you were in dire straits. I want to help you. I never stopped loving you."

"But…but…." Becky started crying again. All this time she believed her father did not love her. He was right about her mother. She was mentally unstable.

"Would you allow me to help you?"

Becky nodded and ill-feelings she had for her father faded away. She needed her father more than he could have ever imagined.

Chapter 68

Newsworthy

For the first time since working for Select Committee for General Services, Paul had a restful night of sleep. He went to bed knowing that he was protected by several FBI agents, who surrounded his house twenty-four, seven. He turned the TV to the local news station. His eyes grew wide after the news anchor reported on a story about a government employee shooting her daughter at Oriole Park. The anchorman also reported that the same employee was involved in a fatal car accident in New York.

Paul reached for his cell phone to call Liz, but she beat him to it. He smiled when he looked the Caller ID before answering her call. "I just heard the news, Liz. I didn't think it would end like this."

"It's crazy how things ended. It's too bad that Eddie Rosenthal and Stephanie McPherson did not live long enough to explain why they cahooted to defraud the government."

"Yeah, I know. Though, I got a feeling Stephanie was the brain behind the scheme. Her file shows she was promoted to Senior Writer three years ago, which happens to be around the same time this scheme started."

Liz nodded in agreement. "I suppose you're right."

"What about Sally Bates and Barrett Pike?" Paul asked out of curiosity. "Any leads on their whereabouts?"

"No luck. It's like they disappeared in thin air. The last cell ping shows Barrett was in West Virginia and Sally was in Maryland. They could be anywhere by now. But we won't stop until we find them, especially Sally. The FBI believes she is the primary suspect in Cyrus Hampton's murder."

"I'm not surprised." Paul replied, thinking he could have been in Cyrus' shoes. "What about Tameka Collins-Brown?"

"She will stay in Witness Protection as long as Sally Bates is nowhere to found. I believe our luck will change after we add her to the FBI's Most Wanted list."

"That's a good idea."

"I can't thank you enough for helping with the embezzlement scheme. I wish you would consider staying at SCG as the Director. We need someone of your caliber to run the Agency."

"Thanks for your vote of confidence. I'll think about it." Paul burst out in laughter after the President disconnected the calling without saying goodbye. *Some things never changed.*

As soon as Paul disconnected the call, Brian showed up at his house with Maria. He looked out of the peephole before opening the front door to let them in. "This is a nice surprise."

Brian smiled. "We just came by to check on you. But based on the black and whites, you are well protected."

Paul snickered at Brian's nickname for the FBI agents. "Yes I am. And this must be Maria," he said as she stood next to Brian.

Maria smiled. "Nice to meet you."

"I heard good things about you."

"Likewise," she replied with a wide smile. "If you don't mind, is it okay if I use your restroom?"

"Sure." Paul pointed while explaining, "It's down the hall to the left."

As soon as Maria was out of sight, Paul said to Brian, "Glad you stopped by. I have some news to share with you."

"Stephanie McPherson died from a car accident," Brian blurted out.

"Yeah, I take it you looked at the news this morning."

"A lil bit. So what's next?"

"Sally Bates is at large. Enough time has passed so she can be in Timbuktu by now. Fortunately, we were able to recover some of the embezzled money."

"But it was only a fraction of the three million dollars that was stolen. I was shocked when you told me the scheme happened over a three-year period."

Paul nodded. "It began the same time Stephanie was promoted from Secretary to Senior Writer."

"Eddie Rosenthal promoted her, correct?"

"Exactly! It's too bad Cyrus Hampton lost his life in search of the truth."

"It could have been worse."

"I know," Paul replied, realizing he could have been the next murder victim. "On a lighter note, have you heard from your brother?"

"Yeah, Charlie's in rehab. It looks like he's ready to commit to change."

"I'm glad to hear that. Make sure you tell he has a job when he gets out."

"Will do. Thanks for everything."

"No problem. You would have done the same for me."

They shook hands as Maria returned from the restroom and resumed her position standing next to Brian.

"Why don't you two stay for lunch?" Paul asked.

"No can do. We are headed to a play in New York. Do you want to tag along?"

"And be a third wheel? No thank you."

Brian chuckled.

"Have fun." Paul shook Brian's hand, then he turned to Maria and gave her a small peck on the cheek. "It's nice to meet you. Hopefully, I'll see more of you."

Maria blushed. "I hope so too."